Reparations USA

PHILIP WYETH

Also by this author:
Reparations Mind
Reparations Core
Reparations Maze
Chasing the Best Days
Hot Ash and the Oasis Defect

Cover design by Philip Wyeth.

www.philipwyeth.com

CONTENTS

1. THE PROGRAM

The studio audience responded to the producer's waving arms by cheering loudly. When the theme music began to fade out, they quieted down. A camera dolly crept toward the bright stage where two women sat opposite one another on red felt chairs.

"Welcome back to *Tina Talk!*"

The host was a lively woman of forty, whose sculpted brown mane flowed onto a bright yellow dress which hugged her curves and showed off much of her long legs, right down to the matching high heels.

"Our guest this segment is Kate Donohugh, and she works at the Historical Reparations Administration megabranch in Newark. Welcome, how are you?"

"Hi, Tina! Thank you so much for having me on."

Kate, who was in her thirties, wore clothing more appropriate for someone speaking on behalf of the government, but was put together in a way that showed she had enough style sense to make any outfit work.

"Now," Tina began, "it says here that you are an Assistant Regional Manager, but isn't it true that you really have to be a jack-of-all-trades considering the kind of work that goes on over at the HRA?"

"That's right. What we do tends to be cross-disciplinary, but at the same time you've got to have the right people skills to interact with the public."

Tina looked down at a pad in her lap and spun a pen in her fingers.

"I'm quite fascinated by all the fields of expertise that came together to make this project even possible. I mean, five-hundred-plus years, that's a lot of people and events to account for!"

"Oh yes, the HRA is an incredible undertaking! In fact, a whole new college career track called Reparology was recently designed to give students a rigorous background in such areas as history—of course, haha—but also accounting, social work, law enforcement, archaeology, genealogy, and—should I keep going?"

Kate gave a smile and the audience responded with a healthy round of applause.

"Hahahahaha, that's remarkable," Tina laughed. "Now, the administration officially launched just two-and-a-half years ago—"

"After nearly a decade of planning, mind you."

"Of course. So you rolled it out across the country, opening field offices for customer service, document submission, appeals… You're a veritable DMV of sorts, hahahaha…"

"Oh yes, the HRA was unprecedented in its goal of righting all the wrongs that piled up ever since that first European ship landed on Tribal American shores. We understood the importance of engaging with the public on a practical level to work toward that goal, because it is an ongoing, perpetually adapting program. At the end of each month our supercomputer network—"

"MARVIN."

"Haha, yes, which stands for Macro Aggregating Restitution Vector Input Navigator. He—it—MARVIN, conducts a rolling audit as new documents come to light, which ensures that those who owe historical debts pay their fair share."

"Fascinating. Now, this can all seem a bit abstract so why don't you give our audience some hard numbers about the results you and the HRA are achieving."

A graphic appeared and Kate began to walk viewers through the charts.

"In just a couple of years we have been able to assist one-hundred-sixty-million Historically Wronged Americans, who fall into our Beneficiary class, by recapturing seven trillion dollars from Legacy Violators, members of the Debtor class which consists of approximately two-hundred-seventy-five-million citizens."

"Is that not amazing, folks?" Tina implored the audience to stand up and clap. "A dot-GOV agency really doing its job, all right!"

After the crowd settled down, Kate continued. "The program has been such a success that—while I can't divulge any specifics—let me just say that we are in negotiations with certain well-known international bodies to roll out sister agencies in Europe and its former colonies. This won't happen overnight, however, because compared to the rest of the world, the United States is a fairly small and well-documented country. Can you imagine the amount of work it will take to just get organized in huge landmasses like Brazil, Africa, and India?"

"Kids watching at home," Tina cackled, "if you're looking for long stable careers where you get to see the world—learn a second language now and get on the

HRA career track!"

"Haha, yes, exactly…"

"Tell me, having made so much progress already, can you predict when the program might achieve its goal here at home?"

"I'd say still quite a while. New documents from the distant past are being discovered every day. These have to be uploaded into the system, processed, and then authenticated. Debit Scores adjust in each monthly spreadsheet to reflect the latest data.

"But beyond redistribution," Kate continued, "our deeper goal is for Beneficiaries to achieve competence and self-sufficiency. And I can report that a small but respectable percentage of them have been using their newfound capital to restore crumbling neighborhoods and start new businesses. Shout out to the HRA jobs training program!"

"Absolutely! Now," Tina said as she furrowed her brow, "one unfortunate by-product of these historical documents taking such a prominent role in our everyday affairs, is the rise of an underground resistance campaign by so-called debt protesters, who make no bones about destroying inconvenient archives."

"Yes, unfortunately the descendants of KKK members who once rode through the night to lynch Afrigro-Americans, now go to great lengths to shirk their responsibilities in this modern-day version of book burning. It is a crime. And not only that, it is a violation of human rights."

The audience rumbled in a low cascade of boos.

"Now, Kate," Tina said. "Let me change gears here to talk about one of the more innovative ways the HRA is spreading its message. They call it Direct Descendant Match—DDM, for short—and it's actually modeled after game shows. Can you please explain?"

"Of course. As your audience knows, our supercomputers are constantly reanalyzing the vast historical database and making new connections. On average, for every thirty billion Certified Historical Events that MARVIN processes, it matches up two living citizens where at least ten Domination Events—DEs—have taken place between their bloodlines in the past five hundred years."

"Can more than one DE within a single lifetime count toward the total?"

"No, and that's what makes DDM so significant. We're talking about ten of Person A's ancestors involved in DEs with ten of Person B's ancestors. Usually the domination is always one-sided, but in rare cases it isn't and MARVIN takes these details into account.

"Anyway, the HRA believes that such heavily weighted bad karma should be redirected in a public forum to help cleanse our national palate. So these two people appear on the show, *DDM TV Live*, to explore the dark and violent path that led them to this dramatic moment."

"Sounds fascinating! Then what happens?"

"Well, MARVIN never stops calculating, and just before he passes assessment, he processes documents from the contestants' own lifetimes."

"Nooooo!"

"Hahaha, yes, it's amazing, I know!"

"And then what?"

"The two join hands, and as they face the screen their assessment is read."

"And it just so happens that you brought us a clip from a recent episode of the show. Let's take a look!"

A video began, showing a skinny white man in a

striped v-neck t-shirt holding hands with a short woman of Northern Tribal features. A deeply suntanned host said, "Jonathan Wibble. Your blood has affronted the blood of Agnes Yazzie sixteen times. No slivers from your bank account could hope to make up for these crimes. In the name of justice and fostering goodwill, so that we can finally stop this cycle of abuse, you are remanded to HRA Garden 2-F in Champaign, Illinois, where you will grow food with Mrs. Yazzie for a period of one year. And afterward, your reduced Debit Score will reflect this honorable service."

The studio audience went wild with applause. Tina leaned forward onto her crossed legs and brought a hand to her heart.

"My goodness," she gushed. "Is that not proof that the HRA is about more than money, and also helping to move humanity forward?"

More applause. Kate mouthed "thank you" to the crowd.

Tina sat back and said, "Kate, it's been a thrill having you here, but before I let you go, one last question. Have any love connections ever blossomed during a DDM assignment? Seems like all those months together, things could get *very* intimate!"

"Well," Kate began with a sigh, "such liaisons are discouraged—because in fact a certain percentage of DDM conflicts do involve family feuds over romantic affairs—but I am happy to report that there are three married couples out there right now thanks to the program."

"How about that, ladies and gentlemen? Kate Donohugh, thank you so much for coming on *Tina Talk*..."

After the show, Kate stepped into the brisk, overcast Manhattan streets with a jump in her step, feeling proud that she'd given the HRA a good showing. She was in no way a trained PR spokeshuman, but between her genuine smile and high school theater background, the administration felt confident in sending her out for the occasional media puff piece.

Aside from a few smaller news programs and prerecorded web spots, however, most of her previous media placements had only been quotes in press releases and news stories. This *Tina* show was by far her biggest appearance, and perhaps normally out of her league, but the HRA was celebrating the latest trillion-dollar milestone by sending out anyone who wasn't a total buffoon to tout the administration's success.

What had started nearly ten years earlier as a disorganized rabble of idealistic left-wing activist groups had tapped into a growing sentiment that beyond merely throwing government money at problems—War on Poverty, War on Drugs—the similarly abstract War for Equity required not only an organized, systematic approach but also an adaptive component. Because when holding history's conquerors to account over such a long timeline, a rigid set of rules would only hamstring the executive body and set the program up for abuse and failure.

This all coincided with the reliable political pendulum swing back to the left after nearly a decade of populist-fueled conservative rule, so that when the reinvigorated Dramacrats won a majority in both houses of Congress, their new president quickly signed into law the establishment of the Historical Reparations Administration. And contrary to the Rebellicans' snide predictions of economic doom, it turned into a jobs bonanza because so many different professions were required for the whole plan to work.

Eileen Jeffries-Lao, the ceiling-shattering candidate who became both the first female and first Chinese-American president, was called a modern-day FDR as an army of document experts, historians, social workers, and accountants all moved in to the administration's seven hundred new field offices, which had employed another thirty-eight-thousand people during construction.

Kate Donohugh's life dovetailed with all of this beautifully. Whereas so many idealistic young people find that the pull of the world's demands slowly suffocates their desire to make a difference, Kate had been among this new breed of digitally empowered activists who had never tasted the good-times wealth that the Boomers and older Gen Xers enjoyed. Children of successive economic avalanches, these late-stage Gen X, Millennial, and Gen Z visionaries used their tech savvy to circumvent the ossified policies of the status quo and mold all the disparate groups that were yelling in the streets into a legitimate political force effecting tectonic policy changes on a national level.

It was not all some hippie fantasy, however. For so many Caucmericans to willingly transform the amorphous concept of "white guilt" into an actionable platform required ruthless introspection so as not to patronize the very Minoricans they sought to help. To do so, they channeled life opportunities stemming from their privileged backgrounds toward a goal which was bigger and more noble than merely helping a homeless person or even one's local community—because the HRA, dollar by dollar, was making a rigorous public accounting of half a millennium of oppression and exploitation, both by clearing the balance sheet for the living as well as setting a tone for how business would be done moving forward. In short, equitably.

Whenever Kate felt the weight of colonialism bearing down on her shoulders, or in moments of prideful weakness, she recited a prayer from the Book of Reparations, the inspirational tome compiled during the years that this political crusade unfolded. "Although I was born into this white vessel," she would whisper, "we all bleed red. No matter how privileged I find my station in life, I extend a hand down so that one day we may all stand side by side."

These words helped Kate keep perspective whenever she felt a pang of guilt about her comfortable life: nice apartment in gentrified Brooklyn, her white husband Chris, and their two Corgis. At least they'd decided not to have kids—that was easy penance for two middle-class Caucs in their early thirties to pay.

Back to reality, Kate mused as she breezed past the retinal scanner at an employee entrance of her HRA field office across the water in Newark. She took an elevator up to the second floor and headed to her desk.

"Great job today," a voice said from below a nearby cubicle wall.

Kate shifted in mid-stride to enter the workspace and received a warm smile from TJ, a plump bearded coworker whom she also considered a friend. He was a reparatician highly skilled in document analysis, particularly in detecting pixel flaws deep within flattened forgeries. This work both reduced MARVIN's workload and kept the payments flowing.

"Everyone's got to pitch in," she said and reached to meet his high-five.

"You're telling me," TJ sighed. "I've been asked to do three radio segments and you know I *never* do these promo things—but at least one's NPR, my fave!"

"Well, it's an election year, and we've got a lot to celebrate, right?"

"On the surface, absolutely. But between you and me, I think the Old Debt Boy Network has finally started to shake off their hangover and get a bit more organized."

"Whaaaat?" Kate leaned in so they could speak discreetly—they were surrounded by wall-mounted cameras that could enable someone reviewing the footage to read their lips, as well as dozens of employee tablets that were equipped to record audio.

TJ lowered his voice and said, "You know that I ran away from the South as fast as my hiney could take me, but I still check in with my folks every so often (Lord knows they're getting up there in age). So anyway, the last time I spoke to my dad... I don't know... Just something about the tone of his voice, it sounded less down in the dumps. And some of the things he said made it seem like he'd even made his peace with me— for being gay *and* working for an organization that he once said was stealing my inheritance.

"So I asked him if he was sick and he clucked, 'No! Doc says I'm fine,' so I said, 'Well, what *is* it, Dad? Don't leave me in the dark.' And he just blew it off, 'No, no. Everything's fine. Seems like this country's headed back on the right track again, that's all.' And I was like, 'Okay, I guess...?' "

Kate made a face. "Weird."

"I know, right? So I jumped online and started poking around for negative chatter about the HRA—at home on a private browser via proxy server, of course; God forbid I did that here—and I've got to tell you, not only are the hate sites saying the usual nasty things, but vandalism on scanners and field offices is up twenty percent in the last six months alone."

"Really? I haven't heard anything about that."

"Wouldn't surprise me if they're trying to keep it all hush-hush. And you know, some people are just up and leaving. They'd rather live off the grid than pay—"

"Ah, here's our big morning show star!" an approaching voice beamed from outside the cubicle.

It was Jan, a regional manager and Kate's direct supervisor—an eighteenth-generation Afrigro-American who donated her benefits to fund summer camping trips for inner city kids who otherwise might never see the countryside.

Jan patted Kate on the back, smiled at TJ, then said, "But as great as you were out there, the trenches beckon. Got the usual drama over in disbursements: lady brought in her kids, wants more money, you know the drill. Asked for a supervisor but honestly, DC scheduled a last-minute conference call that I've got to sit in on. You're senior enough, Ms. *Tina Talk*, think you can handle that for me?"

"But of course," Kate said with a nod and twirl of her hand, smiling at TJ as she drifted away.

No time for lunch today, she thought, her stomach grumbling at each turn down the winding hallway. An elevator ride took her down to the ground floor, then she went out one security door, scanned her key card at the reception entrance, and walked past a dozen cubicles before finally turning right into a small room with a table and four chairs.

Inside, a young black woman was tending to a baby stroller while a boy explored the room.

"Hello there! I'm Kate Donohugh, I hear you asked for a supervisor?"

"Yes, thank you. I'm Myra Jenkins."

"Why don't you take a seat and let's see if I can help

you."

As they sat down on opposite sides of the table, Myra pulled a folder out of her bag and began spreading papers over nearly the entire surface.

"Okay, this is the family tree that I got from y'all." She held up a printout which bore the HRA seal, then picked up a second sheet with her other hand. "Says right here I'm only entitled to six hundred dollars each month for past crimes against my people. But that just ain't enough and we used to get more. I got two little ones. Can you do anything to help us?"

While Ms. Jenkins was saying all this, Kate had removed her laptop from her work bag and opened the lid. As she booted up and logged into the HRA system, she said, "Let me just access your file—"

"The man I talked to at the counter already did that."

"Yes, well, I'd like to get up to speed before answering any of your questions."

As Kate cycled between tabs on the screen—which displayed details about Ms. Jenkins such as her age and address, ancestry, and finances—she felt something hit her foot. She looked down to see a six-year-old boy with a race car in his hand smiling from beneath the table.

"Oh, hello there, young man!"

"Tyrell," Myra sighed, "is that you under there? Please get up and let this woman do her job."

The boy crawled out and she motioned for him to sit next to her.

Kate turned her attention back to the file, which included certain tabs only visible to higher ranking employees—the first case worker did not have access to this information. She tapped a nail on the screen and looked up.

"Okay, I think I see the problem. Earlier this year the MARVIN mainframe accepted two new documents certifying that in 1822, an ancestor on your mother's side purchased two slaves."

"But what's that got to do with me?"

"While black-on-black ownership was uncommon, and oftentimes the result of freed slaves buying their own relatives—*although... actually...* that purchaser was a white farmer named Colin Evers. So it looks like you are, in fact, one-two-hundred-and-fifty-sixth Caucmerican!"

"Wow. Um… So nothing about *my* life has changed—except I had a baby last year—but you found some old piece of paper and now I get less?"

"You've done quite well under the program so far."

Myra looked down into her hands. "I know, but it's hard out there, even with your money."

"It's not *our* money—it's yours!"

"I'm just sayin', couple months back, the landlord started charging a new fee on top of the rent. Called it 'lurf' or something."

"Yes," Kate sighed, "that's the Lower Income Retainer Fee, unfortunately. Property owners have lobbyists too, and they were able to convince the legislature to collect that from many Beneficiaries who rent."

"I see."

"Oh, there's one other thing I should bring to your attention. Informally, of course."

"And what's that?"

Kate rotated her laptop and a small video player showed a black teenager spraying graffiti.

"That's your cousin Alex outside a Shell gas station two weeks ago."

"Why are you showing me this?"

"Because," Kate began, "the Joint Telecom & Penal Bureaus want to implement a new policy where all petty crimes caught on camera with definitive ID—and here we have scans of both Alex's face and eyes—they would bypass our overcrowded court system, and instead fines would be imposed automatically."

"Which means what, exactly?"

"Reduced payments, for one. And the possibility of being placed under Microscopic Protocol."

"What's that, like probation?"

"Precisely," Kate said with as friendly a smile as she could muster. "But the HRA has *begged* these bureaus not to move forward because it will disproportionately affect the people we're trying to help here. But I've heard that they're compiling a large body of evidence they want to present before Congress to try and force it through."

"When's all that gonna happen?"

"If we're lucky we'll hold them off until the beginning of next year. But maybe you can give Alex a little heads-up to be more careful out there."

"So you got these cameras everywhere and you're just watching everything people do?"

Kate pointed to a camera mounted in a protective box up in the corner of the room and winked.

"This ain't right," Myra said as she stood up and gathered her papers in a mash. "I thought the whole point of these agencies was to *help* people. C'mon, Tee, let's get out of here…"

She wheeled the stroller out through the door and Tyrell followed.

Kate eased her laptop shut, walked to the door and quietly closed it, then wedged herself into the corner directly under the camera, trying to be in as little of the frame as possible. She closed her eyes and rubbed circles around her temples while taking slow even breaths through her mouth, then began reciting the Mantra of Atonement. "Although I was born into this white vessel…"

Stressful encounters like these were the biggest cause of burnout on any HRA staff. A platoon of therapists had been trained to specifically address this pressure point, and with soothing words they attempted to reinforce the core idea that the HRA sought an incredibly lofty goal in trying to repair over five hundred years of ugly history, but human nature doesn't simply change overnight. Therefore employees were encouraged to view their role as holy humans leading pilgrims across dangerous and unfamiliar territory into the Promised Land.

A few minutes into the calming routine, Kate heard her work phone ping from inside her bag. It was a text from Jan's assistant which said: "Boss still on conference call. Asked if you'd head over to Debts and help out. Room 114."

Kate wrote back, "Sure thing. Challenges on both sides of the spreadsheet today, what can you do?"

In addition to secure employee-only areas, the public sections of all HRA field offices had separate wings to serve Beneficiaries and Debtors. Smart scanners granted appropriate entry to each side, and armed guards posted throughout the facility helped prevent or break up any conflicts between the two groups.

For Kate to reach the Debtor wing, she had to walk through an exit-only door, wind her way down several bright corridors, then scan herself through an interior employee entrance. This side of the facility had a bit more security on hand, and Kate always felt a slight chill in the air here. Everyone understood that this was not the happiest of places, because even though the dual-purpose field offices had been set up to encourage dialogue with the public, Debtors rarely brought in authentic documents that reduced their obligations or at least warranted an extension.

Not that in-person pleas were the only or most effective means of reducing one's debt load. Legal and accounting firms had virtually tap danced with glee at the immaculate conception of a whole new revenue stream when the HRA was created. Perhaps the most opportunistic company of all was the tax firm H&R Block, which poetically rebranded itself as working to "block" historical reparations from being collected.

Between these scoundrels trying to put the brakes on one of mankind's most noble projects and several legal cases working their way up the court system hierarchy, HRA employees felt enough trepidation below the surface to keep motivated and working on an aggressive timeline. There were so many past examples of ambitious programs that had been derailed by judges or bureaucratic incompetence, that there was simply no room for hubris or believing that the righteousness of one's cause guaranteed the inevitability of its success.

For each day that passed without an injunction granted by some bench that was stacked with Rebellicans during the past two presidential terms, it meant that millions of deserving Americans had been served another small taste of justice.

With these conflicting sensations of apprehension and purpose, Kate smoothed her blouse then stepped resolutely in her pump shoes across the threshold into a room that very much resembled the one she had just left in the opposite wing of the field office. Inside sat a Caucmerican in his sixties with stringy, stark white hair and heavy eyelids over blue-gray eyes. She extended her hand.

"Kate Donohugh, how do you do?"

"Miss, my name is James. I got a bum knee, my truck needs new tires, and my job at the hardware store —which I suspect just keeps me on because I been there for so long—they cut my hours back to just twelve a week."

"I'm sorry to hear all that."

"So how do you expect me to pay?" he asked, letting the last word slowly trail off.

"Well, if you could just tell me your last name," she said while her hands automatically reached for her laptop, "I'll review your account and see what I can do."

The man leaned away and slung an arm over the back of his chair. "Here we go again."

"Full name, please?"

"It's James William Haggerston. I already went through all this. The lady outside scanned my eye with her tablet and everything."

"I know, I know, just give me a second. Yes, there you are. Hmm. It says here you only owe a hundred and thirty dollars per month, that's not so high— especially considering that your great-great-great-great-uncle killed three Choctaw Indians."

"But my actual father managed a furniture factory that hired dozens of Minoricans, as you call them, over the twenty-odd years that he was in charge there. Surely that's got to offset something a distant relative did in the 1850s."

"Thirties, actually. The 1830s."

Silence.

"And yes," Kate continued, "your father's biographical data points have all been uploaded and factored in to your cumulative Debit Score. But there's so much more: at least two ancestors worked on slave ships—granted, they only delivered human cargo to the West Indies, and I don't think the HRA has an extraction treaty there yet—but moving on, I also see theft of indigenous land, and even a case of arson against an Afrigro-American man's tractor."

"My god, are you talking about my cousin Luke? He and Albertson were friends! They used to get drunk together all the time. It was his damn wife that pressed the charges—no one really knows what actually happened!"

"The court documents in my system are pretty unambiguous."

"He said, she said, I don't know what to tell you. He had to pay them damages at the time, right?"

"The point, Mr. Haggerston, is that you felt compelled to come down here to plead your case, and so far you haven't given me much of a reason to even offer you a grace period."

He pulled out a kerchief and wiped his forehead, then said calmly, "I am tired from working my fingers to the bone just trying to survive. First they closed the factories and moved them overseas. Then they let illegal labor come in and undercut my wage. I tried to adapt by learning computers but they change faster than I can keep up. And hell, Burger Citizen started using kiosks to take your order so I can't even work there now.

"It's enough to break any man down, I don't care *what color* he is or who his second cousin, ten times removed, fought a duel with. But *you* care. Hard as it is to live in the here and now, I got the HRA with its teeth latched into my shoulder like a damned zombie on the TV. So what I'm asking for is some sort of mercy or understanding, because I cannot win by fighting this administration all by myself."

After a frozen moment, Kate turned back to her computer and clicked around. Her eyes narrowed and when she had locked onto what she was looking for, she tapped a nail onto the screen.

"Mr. Haggerston, I've got two options for you. First, I see your son Morgan earns a nice salary remodeling homes for environmental compliance, and due to several impressive maternal deductions—that being on your wife's ancestral timeline—he barely owes more than you do each month. I could request to have, say, two-thirds of your debt rotated onto his bill if you think that might be agreeable to him?"

"What's my other option?"

"That four acres of undeveloped land you own in Pennsylvania, I could put a temporary lien on it. Secured by the HRA's long-term trust, to be released when you get back on your feet."

"That's family land. Before permits and paperwork turned construction into a bureaucratic decathlon, that property was very much developed. A lot of love and memories floating above the wild grass out there."

He rose to leave and trudged to the door, looking back as he said, "No, I'll find a way to handle this business myself. Because I will *not* place another old man's burden on my son's shoulders. You have already done quite enough of that."

It was only 2 pm but Kate felt like she had worked a twelve-hour shift. Another common symptom of working at the HRA, and internal policy made generous allowances for leaving the office early. CalmTime was seen as more than a fair trade-off if it aided in employee retention, plus there was a long list of on-call temps, fully trained and ready to fill in during these minor emergencies.

Kate saw her hands moving across the laptop keyboard. The employee app opened, the mouse scrolled onto and clicked the TapOut icon, and a green capital R spun as the system sent pulses to alert some central computer that she was done for the day. She felt herself numbly moving down the hallway toward the exit, then she was on the HRA shuttle bus to the subway, somehow found herself on the right train home, and nearly crawled through the front door of her apartment.

No one was home. Chris was across town helping a client set up a new server and the dogs were at day care —was she supposed to pick them up? She'd figure that out later.

Kate moved absently into the bathroom and started to fill the tub. She closed the door and slowly peeled off her work clothes. She saw herself nude in the full-length mirror hanging on the back of the door and began to sob. When her breath caught, she leaned her head against a forearm high on the door and closed her eyes, bringing the other arm across her chest in a sort of hug. The wave of self-pity that had washed over her subsided just as quickly and was replaced by a sudden hyper-awareness.

Her left hand, which was draped across her right breast, had touched on something. She looked down but saw nothing there. She felt again—there, under the surface, something dense about the size of a pebble. Unmistakable. Terrifying. Too much to deal with on top of everything else. She climbed into the bath, draped a washcloth over her face, and went to sleep.

"Hon?" a voiced called from down the hall. "Are you home?"

The sound of dogs barking, clawing outside the bathroom door. Kate pulled the washcloth from her eyes and squinted around the room. A knock at the door.

"Helloooo?" Chris called out playfully. "Kay, are you in there?"

Mechanically, Kate climbed out of the water and put on her bathrobe. She opened the door and before Chris could say a word, she wrapped him in a wet embrace and wept.

2. THE WORKAROUND

The scanner spit out a piece of paper onto the right side collection tray. A black boy about ten years old held it up under the streetlight and inspected the top right corner. In small red letters was the printed message: "Rejected. Level 9 forgery. Please do not resubmit this document. This scanner is under surveillance. Thank you."

The boy crumpled up the paper and tossed it away, then turned to his friends and said, "Here, give me another one."

A second boy reached into his backpack, poked around, then pulled out a more weathered looking sheet. "Try this," he said. "I spent an hour putting in the wrinkles, then I dripped some soda around the edges."

The first boy took it carefully and held it up to the receiving port on the scanner's left side. The machine sucked it in and the boys waited anxiously as it made little fidgeting noises. When it gave a chirp, the second boy said, "That's good, right?"

"It didn't like the first two, spat 'em right out. It

must be thinking on this one."

"Good. I put that the governor's granddaddy stole a car from us. So maybe we can get us a sweet ride."

The three other younger boys tagging along with them liked this idea, and they all crowded close to the scanner as it finished analyzing the homemade document. When the paper eased out onto the cast-iron collection tray—these machines were built tough—they nearly destroyed it fighting each other to be the one who read the verdict.

The first older boy shouted them down and took the sheet. "Durn," he said. "Still no good." He mashed the paper and tossed it into a pile of similar trash that surrounded the scanner. The second boy dove onto the ground and retrieved his creation, unbunching it and studying the rejection message.

"Only a level 8 fake!" he said happily. "Means I'm getting better at this. One day I'm gonna fool it and y'all be asking me for money."

But the other boys were already walking away so he stuffed the paper back into his bag and ran after them. The scanner remained stoic and inscrutable in their wake, even a few minutes later when someone ran up and spray-painted "out of order" onto its dark chrome body.

A boy in his mid-teens approached the group and called out, "Hey Tyrell, yo mama wants you back."

One of the younger boys reluctantly peeled off and said, "Hi, Clyde. Whatchu been doin'?"

"Gettin' everything ready for the Pigeon Man. He says I keep bringing him these drones, he'll let me use a few for my video."

The younger boy made a silly dance move. "DJ Clydoscope, what-what!"

"Don't you make fun now! I got skills. And eyes. I see what's goin' on up in here. Come on."

Clyde softly grabbed him by the scruff of the neck and they walked a few blocks to a rundown apartment building, then climbed up to the third floor. He pushed open the front door which was cracked, and they walked inside.

"I went in there the other day like you wanted," Myra said, facing a well-built man in white tank undershirt and matching skull cap. "But they wouldn't raise it. Maybe next month we get more."

"Man, but I need to get some of that HRA cheese," he said.

"Hold on." She walked over to the younger boy. "Tyrell, why you ain't answer your phone? Can't be out at night like this, you too young."

Clyde stepped in. "He aight. I look out for you. Right, boy?"

"Yeah," Tyrell said softly. He picked up an open bag of chips from the dining room table. "You da man, Uncle Clyde."

Myra turned back to the man and said, "Wish you'd come over here for more than just money, Octavius. Your baby sleepin' in the other room, if you even care."

"At least I'm here," he snorted. "I ain't seen Tyrell daddy face in years."

"Whateva."

"Yeah, whateva's right. Anyway, I gotta head out, handle some business. Yo, Clyde! You wanna do a little job tonight?"

"Aight," Clyde said.

"Well, come on then. Show these hoes how we do."

Myra put a hand on Clyde's shoulder. "You be careful. You know what I told you."

"Yeah, yeah. Don't get no girl pregnant. Don't get in trouble."

"You just got no idea. Tell Mama I said hi when you get home."

Clyde and Octavius put on their coats and walked outside. Octavius pulled out his phone and typed into it while they walked to his car. It was a speckled crimson early '10s Buick outfitted with custom throwback fins and gold-plated rims imprinted with dollar signs. As they entered traffic, he turned on the stereo and loud music started blasting. Clyde asked who was singing.

"DJ Above Ground," Octavius said. "The king of Bayou Rage-Hop."

"Tight."

"Hell yeah. How you doin' with the music? Got any new beats?"

Clyde looked out the window into the street. "Nah. Working on some ideas though."

"You keep at it. 'Cause you never know. But until then, let's go make some real money now!"

They parked on a side street then walked into a liquor store. Octavius waved to the Korean clerk and said, "Sup, Mr. Joon?" as they passed through to the back. He pushed open a door into the stockroom and they walked past stacks of cardboard boxes all the way to the rear exit, which opened onto an alley. Octavius checked to make sure that the slide-lock was secure.

He set up two folding chairs near the door and said, "You thirsty? Go grab us some Lectrolades."

Clyde walked back into the store and browsed in front of the beverage fridges. He picked out two neon plastic bottles and walked toward the counter, but the clerk waved a hand, saying, "It's okay, it's okay," so he turned back, grabbing a bag of pretzels as he passed into the stockroom.

About fifteen minutes later, while he and Octavius were snacking, a brisk three knocks came at the exit door. Octavius looked through the peephole and then opened the door. A lanky young black man walked in carrying a case of beer.

"You just set that on the floor," Octavius said. "You got the receipt?"

The other man put the case down and handed Octavius a sliver of curled white paper.

"You got your card?"

The man held up a credit card. Octavius glanced between it and the receipt a few times, then grabbed a pen from his ear and made a mark on the receipt. "Aight, we cool." He unzipped a pouch inside his jacket and pulled out a small plastic baggie, handing it and the receipt to the customer.

"My man! Say, you mind if I—?" He pointed at the case of beers.

"All good," Octavius said. "Clyde, get this man a chaser."

Clyde opened the box and pulled out a tall-boy of Noble Gent malt liquor, then handed it over. He heard a crisp crack outside the door just before it closed behind the customer.

"And that's how we do," Octavius said. "Full-service station."

Over the next few hours they did business with twenty other customers. Beer cases stacked up high next to the chairs. A little after 1 am, the store clerk came to the back and had a discussion with Octavius that Clyde had trouble following. He saw them count all the cases of beer, then the clerk made some notes on a small pad before pulling a zip-wallet from his back pocket. He removed several white credit cards and handed them to Octavius.

"Yo, Clyde. Grab a dolly and help this man."

The Korean brought over two dollies from a side wall, and together he and Clyde loaded up all the cases of beer and rolled them back into the front of the store, which was now mostly dark. As they put the beer back into the fridges, the clerk set aside the cases which had been opened and replaced the missing bottles and cans with matching loose beers that he pulled from the refrigerator shelves. He resealed each box with a small glue gun before sliding it across the floor to Clyde.

Octavius came in from the back and said, "Aight, Mr. Joon. See you tomorrow night."

"Okay, see you!"

On the drive back to the neighborhood, Octavius said, "Nice work tonight."

"Cool. I had a good time."

Octavius reached into his pocket and handed Clyde one of the credit cards. "Here ya go. HRA card, all loaded up!"

Clyde took the card and put it into his wallet.

A few minutes later Octavius said, "Drop you at your mom's?"

"Yeah."

"You got my number?"

"Think so."

"Okay. Maybe we do this again."

"Yeah."

When he got out of the car, Clyde turned back and said, "You going back over to my sister's?"

"Nah. Got somewhere to be."

"Oh, okay. Later."

Clyde watched as Octavius gunned the souped-up

Buick around the corner and out of sight. Then he heard the buzz of a mini-drone zipping past, tracking it with his eyes by the green light casting downward as it maneuvered through the streets.

These cylindrical HRA drones were about the size of the average city bird, and equipped to record audio and video as well as summon emergency personnel. They bore a capital *R* underneath, which sent an assuring green glow down onto the residents they served in dangerous neighborhoods densely populated with Beneficiaries.

Clyde thought back to when the HRA had first been signed into law. People danced in the streets in celebration. White HRA reps ran around the neighborhood with questionnaires asking how they could help the residents improve their lives.

Over time these workers slowly disappeared, and in proportion the drones began to appear zipping through the streets. While Clyde could remember in his early childhood seeing cameras mounted high above some of the larger intersections, now you couldn't even walk down an alley without wondering if one of these "birds" wasn't secretly watching from a charging station—which were now installed more discreetly than at the beginning, because kids being kids, they had made a game out of smashing this gear.

A couple of the more enterprising older guys approached the boys and suggested that rather than destroy the drones and chargers, they could earn HRA cards loaded with twenty dollars for every intact item they brought over.

So Clyde spent the afternoons of his adolescent years after school with like-minded mercenaries trying to crack the code on how to bring down the HRA mini-drones without causing damage. It had been relatively easy—and thrilling fun—to destroy them in combat, but to knock them out of the air without breaking their fragile components was a new challenge.

First they had to figure out how to slow them down, preferably getting them to hover in place. They understood that these drones, being an auxiliary of the HRA's mission to improve Beneficiaries' lives, were programmed to respond to sensory data that indicated possible crime, danger, or injury. So Clyde and his friends began simulating robberies and bicycle accidents to get their attention. But once they appeared, the drones never dropped below twenty feet—and simply throwing objects at them wasn't any good now. The boys started to get frustrated knowing that money was sitting on the table if they could just think of a solution.

One day when they were killing time, they saw a real emergency up on someone's balcony. An old woman was screaming for help because her husband was having a heart attack. The boys watched as a mini-drone appeared at her eye level, then hovered for fifteen minutes until the paramedics arrived to take her husband away.

Clyde and his friends, in a moment of glorious abstract clarity, realized that if you targeted a drone from *above* it wouldn't see you coming—then all you had to do was control the way it came down. They started staging their own health panics—best to avoid fake assaults in case the cops actually showed up—on balconies and other places where you could get up onto the roof, and while the drone observed the situation, one of the boys standing above would cast a large blanket over top of it. Then the clump fell down softly onto a large piece of foam that another boy had rolled out to pad the landing. And just like that, they were in business.

You had to be careful handling the drones once captured—their tiny hyperblades could take your fingertip right off if you weren't careful—and some of the newer models had speakers that barked a warning message too. To secure their fresh capture, one boy slowly pulled the blanket back while another—wearing long sleeves, padded gloves, and a clear face shield— placed it into a homemade box equipped with a stolen charging station fed by battery power. Once in its "nest," the drone stopped talking and the blades shut off.

They had the free night classes to thank for this last bit of technical prowess. The HRA, for all its flaws, was at least serious about its "hand up" philosophy, and had established a new vocational program in town which offered complimentary courses to anyone who was interested in learning blue collar skills, such as engine repair, AC installation, and the fine details of working with electronics.

Among the group of student poachers, Clyde's friend Damon had a real aptitude for signal flow and soldering wires, and it was he who designed these mobile charging stations—"bird cages"—which enabled them to discreetly deliver captured drones to their customers.

The most prolific among them was a guy in his thirties they called the Pigeon Man, because he kept his fleet up on the roof of his apartment building. A military veteran who had spent more of his time in the service tinkering rather than fighting, he now reprogrammed the HRA drones to serve the needs of a poor neighborhood's underground economy. Pickup and delivery of drugs, running the numbers, and his own brand of surveillance which he called "private security."

So Clyde only got a few hours of sleep after Octavius dropped him off, because he and Damon were supposed to meet the Pigeon Man and deliver two drones they'd recently captured. They took an early morning bus a few miles down to his building—the innocuously painted plywood boxes resting on their laps—and rode the elevator up to the penthouse before walking up the last flight of stairs to the roof.

The Pigeon Man, whose real name was Nolan, sat in his work shack with sparks flying all around as he modified something. When Clyde and Damon knocked and walked in, he lifted his welding mask and said, "Poachmaster C, Poachmaster D! Good morning."

They set the boxes down and exchanged semi-elaborate handshakes with Nolan, who couldn't contain his excitement about the new delivery and immediately opened the boxes.

"Very nice!" he said. "Newer model. Mm-hmm. Pristine. Excellent work, guys."

He opened a drawer and pulled out two HRA debit cards, slapping one into each of their hands.

"Come on," Nolan said, "let me show you something."

They walked out onto the roof, where the rising sun was shining majestically over the whole city. Nolan went to a long row of tall planter boxes and pushed one aside with his hand, sliding it over like a keyboard shelf. Hidden underneath was part of his fleet, charging silently in the dark until needed. He reached inside, grabbed a wireless controller, and said, "Watch this."

With a flick of a switch, four mini-drones slowly rose, then darted away in formation before swooping back in a swirling dance of synchronized beauty.

"You see," Nolan said over the whir of the blades, "I control all four with the same device, but each one can improv freely inside the radius that I set."

Clyde and Damon nodded their heads.

"Here, Damon. Come give it a try."

Damon took the controller and did as Nolan instructed. The birds rose and dove around them in a graceful mechanical ballet.

"You boys are getting too old to be playing in the streets, stealing these birds. Damon, you've got potential with what that trade school taught you. Probably time you started working for me for real. Serious responsibility, serious money."

While Nolan talked and Damon flew the squadron, Clyde looked out over the city that was now bathed in a soft orange light, the drones passing through his field of vision every few seconds. All this gritty work and talk about big money didn't really interest him. He had poetry inside. Still, every time he tried to open his mouth and say something, he felt like he couldn't breathe. But up here—up here on the roof was where he saw what could be. The clear sky, the endless horizon, a straight shot forward into the unknown—and nothing like the human insects fighting each other in the dingy streets below.

He wanted to say all this and more with his music. Tell the world that his neighborhood was still waist deep in shit. That the HRA was maybe a nice idea but all the Beneficiaries—himself included—had found every way to use, abuse, and milk the program, but not in any way that brought about long-term improvement.

They had workarounds for the cashless system and ended up spending their stipends on the usual waste. And so once again it was only the hustlers, liquor stores, and rim shops that got ahead.

He had come into awareness of the world alongside the birth of the HRA, watching as its bubbly workers left the hood each night back to the safety of their own world. And he came of age under the shadow of the administration's high hopes succumbing to the greed and self-destructiveness that only seemed to have increased with all this newfound money floating around.

If he could make something happen with the music, it wouldn't be just so he could get rich and run away. While a lot of his favorite rappers and singers talked about making it big—living the dream life and traveling around—Clyde didn't want to leave his family or his neighbors behind in misery while he posed for pictures wearing diamonds. He wanted to see his hometown become the safe, clean, less tense place that the HRA had probably set out to make it.

But who was he? Just another kid with no dad around, committing petty crimes that no one pursued. Because the HRA couldn't very well go after the "oppressed people" it was created to help.

He'd have to do something though. Maybe finish that new song which had slowly taken shape over the past few months and was about ready now. Try to capture a snapshot of the suffering that he saw in his world each day, and which the HRA's little scouts seemed to miss as they flew by.

"Guess they got the wrong kind of sensors," he said to himself, watching as Nolan's drones soared and tumbled through the air, their green bulbs removed long ago.

3. CRIMINALS

Shortly after sunset, the family gathered around a campfire that two of the men had built up while the other members unloaded the vehicles. In addition to tents, hiker's packs, and coolers, they also removed a dozen bankers boxes which they placed near the fire pit.

Two school-aged children worked together to carry an old footlocker over to the fire. One of the men patted them on the head, then placed his foot on top of the locker and looked into the flames.

A short while later, after the tents had been assembled and some food cooked over the fire, everyone sat around the pit and began to hum softly. One of the women removed a box lid, tapped it with her fingers affectionately, then began dropping its contents into the fire.

Papers, folders, photos all went in and the flames devoured this easy fuel. When the box was empty, the woman simulated wiping a tear from her eye and bowed toward the fire. A man opened the next box, motioned for a boy to join him, then handed him a folder and nodded. The boy opened the folder and let the contents slide out to be consumed.

The humming grew more soulful as each empty box was tossed away into the darkness. When all that remained was the footlocker, a tall man wearing a plaid shirt tucked into dark jeans rose and stood beside it.

"For three hundred years our family has called this land home. From the cold shores of Massachusetts to the fertile soil of the Plains, out to the pitiless heat of the Southwestern deserts, and back again to these beautiful, tree-capped Pennsylvania hills. The adventurers, the farmers, the craftsmen, and so many more. And like any other American lineage, they rode the ups and downs of life in their time, both decent and flawed, with only God to answer to for their reckoning.

"We kept these papers and relics to remember our heritage, the good and the bad. Whoever could have imagined that programs like the Ancestry Project would come back to bite us all so hard?

"Well, we've done what we had to do to give our children a chance to live without a millstone around their neck. The Haggerstons are survivors, so let's keep our emotions in check and get this last bit over with."

He opened the locker and removed a thick folded cloth which he unfurled in the firelight. A large felt Washington Redskins tapestry rippled in the smoky air as the family's song hit a fever pitch.

Just as the man dipped one end of the tapestry into the fire, three spotlights converged on the group. Everyone went silent and the air was filled with the buzz of three orb-shaped drones which approached, one immediately dropping to just above the fire pit and blasting a mist downward that almost instantly extinguished the flames.

The campers leaped up and scattered, some heading toward the vehicles, others aiming for the woods surrounding the small clearing, and the two other drones split up and zipped after them in pursuit.

Official tools of the History Patrol, these large but agile drones—menacing black orbs made of a durable, textured composite material—were terrorizing enforcers affectionately nicknamed S'more Stoppers by the HRA teams which served alongside and maintained them. These document preservation assets came into heavy use after the President Jeffries-Lao executive order which mandated the installation of SafePlace devices in homes nationwide—similar to smoke detectors, these cutting-edge sensors took high resolution scans of documents before they were burned in fireplaces.

People with something to hide adapted and soon found creative ways to destroy documents. Simulated camping trips were a common ruse employed by these scofflaws with large caches of incriminating data to unload. While financial penalties were harsh if caught, the gambit was seen as worth the risk if one could eliminate thousands of dollars of annual debt per family.

The drone that had put out the fire next secured the contents of the footlocker, then sifted through the ashes for any surviving fragments that could be scanned. The other S'more Stoppers were off chasing down the nine suspects. One darted to the vehicles and quickly punctured a tire on each, then retracted its pointed metallic arm and assessed the scene: there were four adults, all unarmed, scurrying around the cars.

The drone first tasered a man who had picked up a dead branch and swung it, then after he fell in a writhing mass, the orb zipped a few feet away and squirted a glowing blue gel at two of the others—this substance contained the same ingredients as pepper spray—and each only ran a dozen steps before also falling to the ground in agony.

The fourth suspect had crawled under one of the cars and was covering herself with leaves to protect against any gel that might be sprayed. The drone placed a flashing red beacon onto the car's roof and then zoomed off into the woods in pursuit of the other suspects.

At the same time, the human members of this History Patrol unit were moving in now that the drones' video feeds had established the size of the party and their, in this case, lack of firepower. While the drones were equipped with a variety of tools and non-lethal weapons, their human counterparts all carried real firearms.

Two agents—playfully called Graham Cracker and Cracker Jack—were assigned to each S'more Stopper, and now these six men dressed in dark camouflage fanned out through the clearing, the flashlights mounted on their rifles sweeping across the suddenly darkened campsite. One agent ran up to the footlocker and slammed the top shut, yelled into the radio mounted on his wrist, and watched as the drone which had secured the campfire rose and flew off in the direction of the pursuit.

Moments later a boxy black truck pulled up beside the suspects' vehicles. A passenger leaped out and ran over to the fire pit, then dragged the footlocker to the rear of the truck and hoisted it in. He ran back to the pit but was waved away by the other man, who nudged the empty bankers boxes with his boot.

Two other members of the tactical unit had meanwhile dragged the woman under the car out from her hiding place and zip-tied her hands and feet. Then they cuffed the other three who had been taken down— also applying neon yellow balm to the two suffering the effects of the blue gel, until the mixture turned green. One by one they were led into the back of the armored truck.

The pursuit in the wooded area was quickly coming to an end. Three of these five suspects were children who had scrambled behind bushes not far from the clearing, and red beacons were dropped in their vicinity. As the two other drones entered the trees, the full force of the S'more Stoppers stalked their prey, scanning and sending data packets back and forth until they had triangulated upon the two remaining adult fugitives.

Each drone was now pulsing a red light as it crept between the tree trunks. Catching a glimpse of one of the suspects through its heat and motion sensors, the first drone that had entered the woods squirted a burst of the glowing blue gel into the woman's eyes, then moved on when she howled in pain and dropped to her knees.

The last suspect had climbed a tree and now all of the drones converged, hovering around him with their spotlights shining. One drone shot a stream of gel but it had no effect because the man had put on gloves and a ski mask, and hid his face close against the bark.

Down below, several of the tactical agents surrounded the base of the tree and aimed their weapons up at him.

"You'd better come down on your own," one of the agents said. "I don't want to kill you, and if these drones taser you, you're gonna land pretty hard."

The man put out a hand in a gesture of surrender, then slowly eased himself down to the ground. Two officers came up and sprayed the parts of him that were blue with the neutralizing gel, then the team leader yanked off his ski mask and held a scanner up to his eye.

"Good evening, Mr. Morgan Haggerston. Ready to take a ride?"

The suspects were loaded into the back of the armored vehicle, which as it left the scene of the raid was joined by three black SUVs, each transporting a S'more Stopper and its human team.

The Haggerston family members sat in various stages of discomfort, worst off being the man with wild hair who had been tasered. Those who had been gelled still suffered minor irritation which was slowly subsiding. The children were frightened, as much by the raid itself as by seeing their parents so shaken. Only Morgan seemed no worse for wear, and despite the trauma to his family, was in decent spirits.

"Say, Dad," he said. "How you doing?"

The tasered man put a hand to his forehead. "Feels like the arthritis in my knee spread through my whole body."

"It'll be worth it in the long run. Maybe a couple days in jail, higher Debit Score for a while, but the most important thing is that all those documents are gone forever."

"What about the stuff in the locker?" the older man asked, nodding at a steel mesh cage toward the front of this rear compartment, where their footlocker had been secured.

"Mostly symbolic stuff. Still allowed to own a Revolutionary War reenactor's uniform, right?"

"I guess we'll find out."

An hour later the truck came to a stop. It was the middle of the night. The double-doors opened and four armed guards escorted the suspects into an HRA facility, which was a closed police station that had been converted for use by the administration's law enforcement wing. The group staggered into a brightly lit lobby, the adults' hands still zip tied, and the children hugging their legs as they moved along.

The four men watched helplessly as the women and children were then taken out of the room, presumably to a washroom and sleeping quarters. The men did not anticipate getting any such rest tonight.

They were told to sit on a bench in the middle of the room, then a junior officer walked past and scanned each man's right eye with a small device. One by one their Citizen Profiles were projected onto the white wall behind a front counter where two other officers were typing into computers. One of these officers pushed a button on the center of the console and a door in the back of the room buzzed open.

The lead agent from the raid stepped in front of the bench and cracked open a tall soda can, taking a long swig and smacking his lips.

"God, I love the taste of carbonated shit after a camping trip." He laughed and the sound bounced around the room's high walls. "Takes the edge off not being at home with my family. But hey, for every one of you that I catch, it shaves a little bit more off my own Debit Score. Call it an employee stock option, if you will."

He paced slowly in front of the men, two of whom had dropped their heads.

"What's the matter, gentlemen? Starting to regret our latest crimes against humanity?"

"Hey, boss," Morgan said, "I hate to interrupt your big moment, but these men might need some medical attention. And besides, you didn't get a damn thing tonight."

"But I got youuuuuu," the agent said, pointing a finger.

"Then do what the law says you can do. This sad performance of yours has nothing to do with the HRA."

"Me, sad? No, no, no. It's you who's gonna be crying. Because it's off to prison for you, and say bye-bye to the kids because your wives, who acted as accomplices tonight, will be deemed unfit as mothers. I just hope the foster parents teach your children better respect for the law than you have."

"You son of a—"

"Agent Essex," the man said as he strutted away, "process, pack, and ship 'em out."

In a manner of minutes, the men were stood up, had their faces wiped clean and their hair brushed, then lined up in a tight bunch directly in front of the counter. A husky Latiza in her fifties wearing a black robe entered the room and sat on an elevated central chair behind the counter.

"All rise," a junior officer said, "the Honorable Judge Hortencia Rosales presiding."

"Good morning, gentlemen," she said. "Since you seem perplexed, let me explain what's going on. I'm one of the night magistrates. I was just awoken from a wonderful dream having something to do with water skiing—and now we are here. Bailiff, what are the charges?"

"Your Honor, these men stand accused of destroying twelve boxes of historical data, as well as possessing Stigmatized Relics and resisting arrest."

"My, my, my. Accused, what do you say to these charges?"

Morgan took a step forward. "With all due respect, Your Honor, don't we have a right to counsel?"

"Ohhh, I forgot." She pressed a button on the center console and an aqua-tinted hologram appeared beside the men. "This is your lawyer, Mr.—" She consulted her tablet. "—Lawbotov."

"What the hell is this?" Morgan said.

"Like I said, he's your counsel."

"A pastel hologram?"

"A SADA, to be precise. State Appointed Digital Attorney."

"You expect us to win this case with a fake lawyer we've never met before?"

"No, I expect to be back in bed in half an hour."

"But if our lawyer isn't real, why do we have a live judge?"

"Because I'm getting paid! 'My people, my people,' you know."

Morgan shook his head and waved a hand.

The men were found guilty of destruction of historical data, but acquitted on the other charges— their CGI lawyer had at least been competent enough to cast doubt on those allegations. But document destruction was seen as a growing threat across the nation—and the HRA wanted to send a preemptive warning to would-be arsonists living in other former colonial countries—so judges were now throwing the book at offenders.

First, the patriarchal line of the Haggerston family was added to the National Doc Offender Registry, meaning that in the future they could not so much as throw out the paper wrapper of a fast food sandwich without handing it over to an authorized Shred-It agent —this being another company forced to rebrand to survive—who would securely transport it and other documents for inspection by HRA scanners before disposal.

First-time offenders were normally put on

probation, which involved enhanced home monitoring by the similarly retooled ADT, as well as weekly sensitivity training meetings. But the volume of documents the Haggerstons had destroyed, which was proven beyond a reasonable doubt by the number of empty bankers boxes found at the scene, as well as one drone's Sift n' Scan of the ashes, compelled Judge Rosales to adhere to the tougher sentencing laws dubbed "One Match Strike and You're Out."

Their punishment was to each serve a year at a former FEMA facility near the Berkshire Mountains, where they would repay their now incalculable debts to society "in a variety of creative ways," Judge Rosales said with a wink.

Before they were led away to wait for the midday transport bus, James found enough strength to ask, "Will I get to see my grandkids before we go?"

The judge laughed and said, "Did Africans who were kidnapped and bound for the plantation get to give their babies a kiss goodbye? I don't think so! Good night, gentlemen."

While it was happily back to dreamland for the judge, each of the four Haggerston men spent the few remaining hours of darkness alone in a cell, sleepless, with tears welling in their eyes. By late morning they were all shackled and loaded onto a bus that had arrived half full, and it meandered through miles of beautiful country roads, stopping twice to pick up more inmates, before arriving in late afternoon at a facility surrounded by chain-link fence topped with razor wire. Two guard towers loomed at the edges, and as the bus approached the entry booth, a large sign came into view that said:

Pennsylvania Debtors' Prison

Rehabilitation Today, Reparations Every Day

After the bus pulled through the gates, the Haggerstons could see that the prison looked more like a work camp, with a handful of narrow, one-story dormitories, two larger administration-type buildings, and ample open space peppered with a number of square concrete plots whose purpose was hard to distinguish in the fading light. A couple dozen inmates were idling around the doors of the living quarters, while others seemed to be flowing into one of the larger structures which cast bright light out of its windows and open double-doors.

The bus stopped in a cul-de-sac near the other administration building, and after the door was opened, the thirty new arrivals shuffled and clanked their way from their seats out into the cool evening air, then through the building's front entrance. None of them spoke or made any shows of bravado—they were not career criminals (not in this lifetime, at least), and it didn't occur to them that they would be watched when approaching a prison yard for the first time.

The processing area was a long open room with various desks, cabinets, and other tools for admitting new inmates. Guards maneuvered the mass of bodies into neat rows, then one by one the men were called up to the front table for the obligatory retinal scan. Each was then escorted to one of the screened off sections in the far corner, where they exchanged their street clothes for prison garb, which consisted of navy blue twill shirt and pants, each bearing a white spray-painted stencil with the letters "PDP."

When admitting was complete and the men were taken over to housing, the Haggerstons found that each had been assigned to a different dormitory. Besides James and his son Morgan, there was also James's younger brother Ed, and Morgan's brother-in-law Gary (whose last name was Olsen, so technically not a Haggerston, but most definitely in the same troubled boat with them). They all passed another restless night, this time among rows of army cots that were alive with the sound of snoring.

Wake-up call was at 6 am, and the prisoners drowsily made their way to the mess hall, which was the other large building that the new arrivals had seen people entering the previous night. The food was tolerably horrible, but the Haggerston clan was at least able to sit together and acclimate to their new surroundings in relative safety. Here they took stock of the prison population: about 250 in all, they were almost exclusively white men except for a few of mixed-race. Judging by appearances, the inmates ranged across all ages and socioeconomic backgrounds, with members of similar classes seeming to stick together. There wasn't any noticeable tension between or hierarchy within these groups either—everyone looked like they were enduring this time away from home in as familiar company as possible.

After breakfast the prisoners went out into the open yard, splitting up and gathering at the many paved squares that the Haggerstons assumed were work stations having something to do with their rehabilitation. Stepping onto the concrete edge of one, they were startled to see a group of men sitting around a table where each was intently focused on a coloring book. Brown and red crayons of various shades were littered across the tabletop, and the prisoners carefully selected each new implement before returning to their work.

James leaned over one man's shoulder and made an admiring remark, then asked, "May I?" The other man smiled and proudly handed over his book. James held it up and flipped through, and the Haggerstons saw page after page of dark brown men driving, red women dancing, milk chocolate children swimming, and crimson boys playing baseball.

James absently handed the coloring book back to the man and then the four stumbled over to another assembly nearby. Here stood a replica Aztec pyramid, about four feet in height, made out of wood and painted charcoal gray. A handful of prisoners sat cross-legged near the base, while two others stood just behind the pyramid, each holding a white and brown Ken doll in their hands.

"Oh, great sky gods of justice," the man on the left proclaimed while shaking his brown Ken, "today we honor your thirst for punishment. Commence the sacrifice!"

The other man placed his white Ken down on top of the altar, then together the two brown Kens did a violent dance which sent the doomed white doll tumbling down the front steps and clattering onto the concrete below. The men who were sitting scrambled forward and fought over the body, while the executioners above made ritual pronouncements that did not bode well for the second white doll.

The Haggerstons turned away without a word, separating as each walked over to another cluster of prisoners. Twenty minutes later they found each other and stared around in bewilderment. A voice came at them from behind.

"Don't tell me you're already shell-shocked! You haven't even heard your first sermon yet."

A muscular man of medium height with slicked-back dark hair approached, holding his hands up to indicate he was not a threat, because there were four of them and this *was* still a prison.

"My name's Aaron, but people call me Brick. I'm guessing this is your first time in rehab?"

"Morgan. How you doing? We're still stunned by what's happened in the past two days. Separated from our families, put in these prison clothes—"

"And now this," Brick said, jerking his thumb toward a group of prisoners.

"Yeah. I just saw three grown men crawl into a tepee together."

"Jesus H. Christ," James said.

"Well, gents," Brick said as he put his hands in his pockets, "that's just the appetizer. I'll look for you after the sermon to find out if you haven't seen the light." He slowly walked away on the heels of his boots.

Ed took James by the sleeve. "What the hell do you think he's talking about? Is this a prison or a loony bin?"

"Looks like we're about to find out," Gary said, pointing to the middle of the open yard.

They could see a tall flatbed cart with large wagon wheels being pulled by a team of four white men in leather harnesses and chains. All the prisoners had dropped their work and were streaming toward it. Standing atop the cart was a rotund black man holding a giant object with some sort of pointed shape.

The Haggerstons looked at each other, took a breath, then walked over to see what would happen next. By the time the cart stopped and they'd caught up to the edge of the large crowd, the black man had set down his prop and was milling around the makeshift stage, which stood about five feet above the ground. He rubbed his hands together and flexed his facial muscles back and forth. Several prisoners up front were so excited that they pretended to box with each other.

Finally the man slid his hands back across the

sparse long hairs on his head, toyed with his wisp of a goatee, then commenced.

"Oh, Lord. A prison yard full of white men. Ain't that a beautiful sight?"

"Amen, yes it is, brother!" shouted one of the prisoners near the cart.

"I *had* a dream—and now it has come true! For the love of God, are *any* of you really surprised to find yourselves locked up in here?"

"No, sir!"

"For four hundred years your families have been kickin', cheatin', sellin', and killin' my people. But *you* thought you was different. 'Those are sins of the past, pal. That's not who we are.' That's what you said. No, no, no!"

He was working up into a sweaty lather of emotion and indignation, stalking around the cart surrounded by a sea of navy blue.

"Something *has* changed though. But it wasn't you, no sir. Know what it was? The law! The law is what changed. And now you are behind bars because you're just like your daddy and his daddy and his daddy before him."

"So what can we do?" another man called out.

"It's a looooong road to Reparations, my friends. But you can start by taking this first step."

"What is it? Tell us!"

The man bent over and hoisted up his prop, swinging it around to reveal a giant check mark. He smiled.

"Check this out. You got to check it, baby. Keep yourself in check. Don't write any bad checks. But most of all, you've got to check your privileeeeeeeege!!!"

This brought a roar from much of the audience.

"Come on, now! Let me see it. Show me how you check your privilege, prisoners!"

The men responded by swarming into a crowded line that extended in front of the cart. The speaker yelled, "Acolytes, forward!" and his team of human horses began to pull ahead. As the cart approached, many of the men stuck out a foot or placed their fingers in the path of the wagon wheels. One by one they turned away hobbling or squeezing their hands with a grimace. Some prisoners who had been blocked when it rolled by now ran up behind and bonked their foreheads against the cart's metal frame, staggering away with mad smiles on their faces.

The Haggerston quartet stood in silent horror as the mob chased after the cart until it reached the main gate, where armed guards stepped forward to disperse the prisoners before letting the black man roll off the property.

Brick slid into view and whistled.

"It's been *quite* a day for you boys. Anybody want to play Barbie?"

"What in the holy hell?" was all that Morgan could muster.

"You just witnessed the soul-saving spectacle of the Reverend Matthias G. Witherspoon, leader of the Foundation for Healing Colonial Guilt."

"And he comes here every day as part of our rehab?"

"My god," Gary added, "they're trying to brainwash us!"

"Depends how tough you are mentally," Brick said. "But no, he only comes here once every couple weeks. He speaks at the other HRA Debtor prisons in Pennsylvania, Ohio, Michigan, and Indiana."

"Tell me this," Morgan said. "If everyone else in

here has lost their mind, why not you?"

Brick gave a little smile. "Because I'm one-thirty-second Navajo? Nah. Maybe some of the guys you see are just playing it up for the yard cameras hoping Rehabilitation Officers will let them out of here early. But hey, meet me and my crew over by the pyramid tonight after dinner." He wandered off in the direction of some of the other new arrivals.

As the day wore on, the Haggerstons fell into a daze watching the bizarre scenes unfolding out in the yard, as prisoners politely rotated from station to station every half hour. A number of inmates emerged from the processing center's side door with white bandages around their injured hands and feet, then rejoined the group activities.

Morgan and Gary took a walk while James and Ed sat down in the grass shaking their heads in disbelief. Gary wanted to talk to a few of the guards and see what their attitude was, because if they were going to live in this madhouse for a year it would be best to get the full lay of the land now.

They found a guard standing next to a water fountain who appeared to be descended from First India.

"Excuse me," Morgan said, "but do you mind if we ask you a few questions?"

"Most certainly, sir," the guard said in an upper-crust British accent.

"Wait a second, you're not American? Is that even legal, for you to work at a federal prison?"

"Funny that a man in your position would be so concerned about legalities. But to answer your query, I was brought to the States several months ago on an H-1R visa in anticipation of a similar Reparations program launching in my home country."

"Oh my god," Gary said, "they're taking this thing worldwide."

"Yes," the guard added, "and India has over one-and-a-half-billion people. The task of getting organized would be overwhelming if not for the excellent training that I and nearly three hundred other Indian team leaders are receiving in the States right now. Next month I shall be transferred to St. Louis to learn how field offices operate. I am very excited!"

"How many of the guards here are in training like you?"

"Only one or two. The rest are real-deal, American-born law enforcement personnel."

"Okay then."

Morgan and Gary made their way to a white guard and said hello. They noticed that he, like about half the other guards, was not armed with a weapon but wore a bulky gunmetal contraption on his right wrist.

"Sir," Morgan said while nodding downward, "is that some sort of weapon?"

"You got it, and then some. Taser, pepper spray, radio, panic button. And it counts my steps. Right now I'm up to... thirty-five hundred for the day."

"You worked here long?"

"This place opened up about eight months ago. I've been here since the beginning. Got my Debit Score down fifteen percent already. I figure another year and my daughter might be allowed to go to college."

Morgan and Gary exchanged a quizzical look.

"What does that mean?" Morgan asked. "I thought some states already gave free tuition to residents—and that was even before this president."

"Sir, that used to be the case, but they did a study to find out why forty percent more women go to college than men. Turns out it was *white* women who made all that difference. So now it's mandatory to fill more spaces with women of color—foreign *and* domestic."

"Well, damn. What's your daughter gonna do if she can't go?"

"Probably follow in her cousin Tammy's footsteps and join the RETC—Reparations Evading Tactical Collectors. We're talking paramilitary, JAG, boots-on-the-ground asset seizure and document preservation kind of stuff. I gotta say, the HRA is turning into a growth industry for us military types. So maybe it'll be better for her. Hell, like the posters say: See the world, save the past, and kick some ass!"

"What do you mean, 'see the world'?" Morgan said. "Don't tell me the HRA already launched overseas!"

"Nah, but you don't think the old colonies don't see it coming? Tammy told us how back in training the instructor showed them satellite temperature data from up in Canada. Buddy—fires everywhere. They're burning documents like crazy trying to protect the Queen. But not anymore. RETC is dropping in like Chuck Norris. Docu Force and shit! Yeah, Tammy!"

He raised his forearm to give a bump, but when neither Morgan nor Gary responded, he said, "C'mon guys, don't leave me hanging…"

Gary reluctantly raised his arm. The guard was so fired up that he slammed their arms together with such power that it triggered his wristband to shoot a taser blast back into his face. He fell to the ground twitching and writhing in pain, which then caused the wristband to send out a distress call to the prison's central computer system. A loud alarm sounded throughout the yard, and a robotic voice blared through speakers up on telephone poles, "Officer down! Disperse and secure!"

The other prisoners began to scatter in panic as the guards who had previously been lounging inside the administration building spread out into riot-containing formation. Several drones also fell in to assist the officers who were already in the yard. With over two hundred prisoners to contend with, their priority was to first rescue the fallen guard, and only then try to herd the men back into the dorms.

Morgan and Gary had immediately backed away from the self-tasering guard, and moments later Brick ran up to them with five other prisoners. "Quick," he said, "find your other guys and follow me. We're getting out of here!"

As they ran toward the mess hall, Morgan turned back and saw his father and uncle coming toward them as fast as they could. Behind them was a mass of men kicking up dust as they swarmed around the yard, with drones and officers trying to steer them far away from the wounded guard. "Hurry up!" he called.

The older men caught up to the group as it slowly crept around the corner of the mess hall. They froze when they reached the back of the building and saw two guards with a menacing black orb hovering between them. Brick gave them a wave.

"You told us you wanted to wait until it was dark," one of the guards said.

"Hell, an opportunity came up. We had to go for it. You ready?"

"Unlock and unload!"

The group ran toward the perimeter fence a hundred feet behind the mess hall. The drone was moving alongside them and fired something toward the barrier. The object landed a few feet short then popped and hissed, quickly filling the area with gray smoke. The men poured into the expanding cloud then watched as the drone approached the fence, lowered itself, and shot out two arms which began shredding the chain links. A few seconds later there was a hole large enough for a man to crawl through.

"Off you go," one of the guards said through the mist. "Take care of business!"

"Damn the HRA," Brick grunted.

The Haggerston men kept their mouths shut and just tried to keep pace with the other escapees, who were in shape and seemed to be coordinating silently—as if this moment had been in the works for some time. First they ran into the nearest thicket of trees before swinging around to one side, running almost parallel to the prison for a few hundred yards, before reaching a thin dirt path that was mostly overgrown.

Leading the way, Brick began to sprint down this path and the others followed rapidly one by one. After a quarter mile, it opened up onto a clearing which revealed a rocky descent, and without a word the men all began to climb down the jagged terrain, steadily working to the bottom a hundred feet below.

Once they reached flat ground, they ran another two hundred yards towards an old beige-and-wood-grain Winnebago that was parked in the shade. Brick banged on the side of the camper. Seconds later a man's head popped out of the driver's window, along with a hand aiming a pistol.

"Holy shit, you guys are way early!" he said, lowering the gun.

Brick gave a grin. "Couple of the newbies unleashed hell out on the yard. We didn't even have to set the fires."

"Good thing you told me to get a big camper. Looks like there's more than five here with you."

"Hell, I couldn't leave 'em behind, right?" Brick gave Morgan a nod.

The escapees piled into the Winnebago and fell

upon a case of water bottles that was on the dining nook table. Then, as the driver pulled onto a dirt road that snaked through the valley, the men swapped out their prison uniforms for street clothes packed into suitcases. Now they began to smile and relax, lounging on couch cushions and on the floor.

Brick, who hadn't yet changed outfits, was hunkered low up front talking to the driver for the first few minutes. He sauntered to the back with a huge grin and let out a whoop. The other men responded with applause.

"Gentlemen," he said, "we did it!"

"Yeah!" they roared.

"Got out of that madhouse. But this was the easy part. Now we're onto the real work of getting rid of the HRA!"

"Hell yeah! Woooo!"

"But," he said, turning to the Haggerstons, "there's just one question I have for the newcomers. Do you enlist?"

Morgan stood up and said, "Two days ago my wife and children were taken from me. If that's the endgame of this whole program, then the government can kiss my ass!"

The group yelled approvingly and Brick met Morgan with a high-five-forearm-handshake that ended in a chest bump.

"Let me fill you in on what you've just gotten yourselves into."

After Brick distributed several laptops to the others in back, he sat down around the nook with Morgan, James, Ed, and Gary, and told them about the underground protest movement which had been growing over the past year.

"Once everyday people started to realize that this

wasn't some temporary thing like they sold it to us—
you know, 'We just want to make sure everybody's
water bottle is full before we keep hiking,' " he said in
a nasally voice, "—and especially when the HRA itself
started dropping hints that they were setting their sights
on England, Spain, France… You know, where does it
end? Should we really let a computer tell a guy who
was born in Canada, and his ancestors came from
Europe, that he owes money to people of a different
skin color—even though their own families maybe
didn't leave the Caribbean until fifteen years ago? It's
crazy."

James spoke up. "I've tried to talk to these HRA
types. For people so obsessed with small details, as
individuals they're incapable of putting down the
script."

"Well, you know, it's gonna fall apart and it's their
own damn fault. Because there's policy, and then
there's reality."

"They seem pretty confident to me. What's their
weakness?"

"Law enforcement, man. The people in the big
cities who cook up all this shit, they think the cops are
all dumb, order-taking robots. A lot of them, yeah—but
enough are awake! They've got kids, bills, and
dangerous responsibilities—do that for a while and
pretty soon you'll know what's what. So I'm telling you,
on the surface the HRA folks are feeling pretty good—
watching everything expand, they think they've never
been stronger. But they're hollow inside! Got no real
support where it matters, and one day—" He jabbed a
finger sideways. "—pop. It'll just stop."

Gary leaned in on his elbows and said, "But won't
that just leave things worse than before? The Bennies
ain't ready to have their stipends cut off. And us

Debtors, well, let's just say *pissed* is a nice way of describing how we feel."

"You're right. And that's why this hasn't turned into a shooting war already. If we can end this thing, we've got to replace it with something better. Which is the reason we need your help now. Because they screwed up not consulting salt-of-the-earth people the last time, and slowly all their theories are turning into a tangled up mess. Do you think seven, eight years ago these Reparations kids envisioned that they'd be sending fellow Americans to prison camps? Hell no! They thought they were just carefully arranging pillows on the couch to make everything look nice and neat."

"Amazing how much damage people who act so friendly to your face can do," Gary said.

"Ain't that the truth. People who've never done a day of manual labor in their lives, let alone had a fist fight to work something out—*they* put *you* in jail! Think about that! But like I said, enough of the good guys ain't stupid. Right now they're just biding their time, all around the country. It's almost game time and we've got a great squad."

Ed pounded his fist on the table. "Put me in, coach!"

The Winnebago moved from country roads to two-lane highways. As the fugitives lay down to sleep, Morgan Haggerston looked at the ceiling and pictured his children's faces. Whatever the underground needed him to do, he would be up to the task if it meant holding them in his arms again.

4. PRIVILEGE

The most frustrating aspect of fighting this disease was the stillness. For the past fifteen years, ever since Kate entered the world of activism as a college freshperson, life had been a wild romantic blur of dashing from scenes of environmental disaster and racial injustice to strategic meetings in rec centers and politicians' offices.

Even in later years, when the HRA concept went from pipe dream to viable to inevitable, and action shifted away from marching in the streets to endless sessions compiling and revising the seventeen hundred pages of the proposed law's guts, days sped by borne on a wing of purposeful mission. Kate could feel the transition from mere activist to bona fide change agent in every fiber of her being with each milestone.

So now, being forced to leave her coworkers and the project behind to focus on her health left her in an existential fog. That daily injection of mental adrenaline she felt before entering the fray to interact with Beneficiaries and Debtors, coordinate with team leaders across the country, and lay the groundwork for the worldwide roll out—now unnecessary as weeks crept by at a snail's pace with seemingly nothing to do between radiation treatments. She knew she should be thankful that early detection had helped her to avoid chemotherapy, but she still found herself lethargic for days at a time.

She had resisted stepping away, of course.

"Maybe I can work remotely," she'd said to Jan. "Do as much as possible to help out."

"Girl, you're sick! Right now you've got to focus on *you* and be with your family. Besides, that next launch pad is still a long way off—get well now so we can press the button together."

"I know, I know…"

With all this down time, Kate suddenly found herself nagged by an old ghost from the early days of her awakening, when the naive, self-centered girl from the suburbs was first bombarded by the raw truth of how overwhelming the scale of world suffering was— pain that was in fact so often caused by other white people.

This new perspective had given birth to an unsparing inner voice that turned making even routine decisions into a statistical analysis ritual, which involved going down a mental checklist to consider how anything she was about to do might affect someone less fortunate than her. It was hard to be present and mindful with so many thoughts pinballing around her head, but Kate made peace with the process by assigning herself an act of contrition or charity to offset any experience or purchase that was pleasurable to herself, such as a kiss or a glass of wine.

This pestering voice went silent sometime during the HRA's planning phase, and was mostly forgotten in the busy and effective years since its launch—a fitting reward considering that Kate and her fellow visionaries had found a way to transmute the chatterbox of one's guilty conscience into applied, outcome-based altruism.

But now, laid up at home with nothing to do, the voice came back maniacally, seemingly oblivious to all that she'd accomplished, and making wild new demands about remedying problems not covered under the HRA's umbrella. She felt her mind short-circuit as it grappled with accusations that she was neglecting these other important human rights issues. How did she intend to help people with gender confusion? Was she a self-serving hypocrite for taking advantage of the HRA's generous health care plan when so many of the people she had allegedly vowed to help still only had access to woeful clinics? Maybe Myra Jenkins was right and the HRA did need to do more.

Sweating alone in bed one evening, Kate tangled her mind in knots trying to think of new ways she could eradicate her privilege. For years she and every white person she knew had done everything in their power to be conscious of their own inherent advantages, and this had guided them daily in trying to help the people who had not fared as well in life's lottery. But now she was beginning to suspect that no matter what selfless act she performed, there would always be something else to account for—and how could you sleep peacefully, let alone function, when the goalposts kept moving?

She turned on the TV to calm herself down, but the first thing she saw was an obnoxious ad by H&R Block boasting about all the archaeologists, translators, and friendly tribal leaders they'd hired to find extra deductions for Debtors. *These guys just won't stop,* she thought—and then the power abruptly cut out and she was left in complete darkness.

She should have embraced this sudden gift of quiet and stillness to go back to sleep, but the old restless Kate of indefatigable action now fighting for her life insisted upon at least getting the flashlight to keep handy until the power returned or Chris got home from the gym, whichever came first. She slid out from the sheets down onto the floor, then delicately crawled over to the TV stand where she groped around the shelves until finding the flashlight.

But she couldn't bring herself to turn it on. The instant she'd grabbed it, her mind envisioned all the people out there who didn't have a flashlight of their own. The inner voice whispered, "Don't use it. Stand in solidarity with them. Check your light privilege!"

From here her thoughts tumbled into a self-incriminating house of mirrors. What *other* comforts did she enjoy without ever acknowledging, let alone act upon to rectify? "Plumbing!" the voice yelled. "Refrigeration! Transportation! Cell phone!" And up until five minutes ago, electricity.

How could she possibly atone for all of this? What virtuous acts would serve to fully exorcise the guilt she now felt for passing decades of her life blind to the thousand micro-advantages she had taken for granted?

Falling deeper into the hallucination now, Kate's mind seized upon the fate of her remains. Although she had already decided that scattering her ashes was preferable to the environmental impact of an ornate coffin or even burying an urn, sudden panic set in when she realized that the energy expended during cremation would still add to her life's cumulative carbon footprint. She fantasized that there must be a way to eclipse the camper's motto of pack-it-in, pack-it-out, and to honor Mother Earth by disposing of a human body so efficiently as to leave no trace—even less than ashes.

Chris found her on the floor cradling the flashlight in the dark. She was paralyzed, couldn't understand what he was saying, but felt him pick her up and carry her onto the bed. She felt the blankets cover her and fell asleep as her body nestled around the unused flashlight.

That night Kate truly believed for the first time that she was going to die. In truth, it was the turning point in her recovery. Dipping a toe into the darkest corners of her subconscious had given her a sixth-sense insight into the many layers and subtle nuances crammed into that word *privilege*, and now her drive to fight for the underdog was ten times stronger than before. Once her body healed, she knew that nothing would ever slow her down again.

5. THE MENTOR

"Clyde! What the hell you looking at?"

Nolan ran up and put his arm around Clyde's shoulders.

"Come on. You got to stay focused. Every time you look over at someone, the camera sees that."

"Damn," Clyde muttered. "I'm just thinking about all this stuff. Like where I got to stand, trying to match the words, you know."

"Just remember, we're cutting this thing together piece by piece. Give me a few good seconds at a time. The action is always jumping to something else."

"Okay. Keep it simple—focus for five seconds, then do it again."

"You're the star. I'm just trying to make you look good!"

Nolan ran back to his computer setup under the tree. A couple of Clyde's friends lounging nearby were providing "security" for the set, which was a small park with an open grassy area near the playground.

"Okay, rolling…" Nolan said, then tapped the screen

of his laptop. "Playback!" He reached for a tablet which was connected to speakers and a rap song began playing. "Action!"

Clyde started moving his body to the rhythm, throwing out his hands and mouthing the words while two of the HRA mini-drones cycled around in front of him. A handful of park visitors had stopped to watch, but he kept his eyes focused on one of the drones, then every few seconds pivoted to face the other.

"Just got paid, by the HRA, wish it was cash, but we work around, work around. Liquor man, double-dippin' his cans, there's a brutha out back, with the workaround, workaround..."

"Cut! Good stuff, young man!"

Throughout the whole video shoot, from early morning takes up on the roof to shots filmed at midnight in the middle of an empty street, and now here in the park, Nolan had been like a kid on his birthday playing with all his new toys. But as a man who truly loved the process as much as the final result, it was unlocking the secret of how to get DJ Clydoscope to perform in front of the camera that really hooked Nolan on making music videos. He would definitely be adding "director" to the list of services offered on his interactive business card.

He ran up to Clyde with a big smile. "We're so close, my man. A few more takes here, then we drive around the hood to pick up some B-roll, maybe grab a few still shots of you—then, I say we're done."

"Cool, cool."

One of Clyde's friends walked up. "Hey, why he ain't ever holdin' up a piece?"

"Because, Stephon," Nolan said, "this ain't that kind of song."

"But he out here representin' the neighborhood.

People gonna see it and I don't want no one thinking we weak."

"My brother. You want to make a video, I will personally film it and you can wave a gun around the whole time."

"Aight! 'Cause I got one on me right now, you know."

Clyde brushed him off. "Stop being stupid, yo! Sun's going down soon, let's get back to work."

Nolan smiled. "Someone gets it. Here we go…"

Clyde had spent the past few months leading up to this music video shoot obeying Nolan's every word. One of the few men he knew who seemed to still be struggling *on top* of the bull—and not scrambling away from it down in the dirt—Nolan was part father figure, mentor, and friend to any kid who was willing to put his guard down and listen.

After Nolan had tapped fellow drone thief Damon to be one of his lieutenants, Clyde found the courage to call on him a few days later and explain what was on his mind. That he didn't want to just *talk* about doing music anymore—he'd already gone through more stage names than written actual songs—and now he had some lyrics he really cared about.

Nolan explained to Clyde some of the lessons he'd learned in the army, most importantly that to get something done you had to make a step-by-step plan and then execute it. "These guys you see on the corner," he'd said, "they get urges every five minutes and think when they chase after whatever it is, that that's a plan. Nah. Let me show you what Uncle Sam taught me."

Nolan told Clyde to send over raw demos of the new track. He blasted back with ruthless critiques but ended each message by saying, "Don't take it personal.

This is how you get better now so that one day you can be great."

Clyde resisted the instinct to lash out at Nolan for dissing his vocals, and ended up putting in ten times more effort recording it than if he'd just done it on his own. But he had to admit, the extra time spent was making the track sound closer to how he heard it in his head.

And then one day Nolan wrote back saying, "You're ready. Let me feed the birds. It's showtime!"

But Clyde started to get nervous after that. It was all theory up until now, but soon people in the hood were actually going to see his video. What would they say? That he was complaining too much about life on the street? And the chorus—the chorus. He thought it was inspiring, the whole reason for the song in the first place—but he wondered if some people might call him soft.

Again, it was Nolan who kept him on task. There were locations to scout, favors to ask from friends, and Clyde had to make a battle plan for the release. His assignment was to research not just the mainstream sites for distributing the single, but get familiar with the hip-hop podcasts in cities with big urban populations like Chicago, Atlanta, and Philadelphia. Get ready to spread the word that a new voice was dropping some unprecedented truth, because *no one* in the scene was holding the HRA's feet to the fire.

Meanwhile Nolan kept busy taking a real-time crash course in music video editing, working late into the night to bring Clyde's vision to life. Gritty street scenes during the verses transitioned to a rooftop at dawn, where Clyde sang the chorus as drones danced around him. "This is getting pretty good," Nolan said to himself.

When Clyde purchased the universal music distribution license through Tunazon, it included a Beneficiary discount, which made him laugh a little. He also prepared what Nolan called the stealth campaign: finding respected sites like Hip Hop Warfare and KeepItTrue to post streaming links, and hopefully get people discussing the song's groundbreaking message.

"Because it ain't the police or white people keeping us down anymore," Nolan had snapped. "And the damn Reparations ain't helping, just like you're saying. It created lots of office jobs for clueless Caucs, but that's about it. Patting themselves on the back with awards ceremonies and luncheons—a million miles away from understanding what's going on across town."

At first Clyde was kind of shocked to see Nolan lose his cool—not many people saw the true inner workings of this disciplined military man—but it was reassuring to know he was human. Nolan was sharp enough to get out of the hood if he really wanted to, and some people wondered why he stuck around when he could play the game. One day as they were watching a near-final cut of the video, Clyde couldn't resist the temptation to ask.

"I'm from the streets, man," Nolan said. "It's in my blood. Sure, Uncle Sam showed me the world but, you know, I care about my people here. And what you saying with this song, I've felt it for years but could never find the right words. But hey, you got the gift!"

Three weeks after the shoot and everything was ready. Clyde took out his checklist and logged into his accounts, then made the release official site by site. It was now time for DJ Clydoscope to engage.

"Okay, here we go."

6. ABSOLUTION

Morgan leaned against a railing in the walkway outside the cuisine court. He could hear the crowd in the main gallery down below, as hundreds of people gathered in front of a stage flanked by glittering blue and silver banners. He glanced back to watch them for a moment, then carefully scanned the dining area and nearby stores. His eye caught on someone stooping over a water fountain, but when that person came out from under the mesh drape, Morgan saw that it was not the man he was looking for.

The crowd stopped chattering and began to "Mmm" in unison. Someone on stage was approaching in a metallic blue-and-silver costume that rose above the head and was squared off at the top and bottom, so that it seemed as if a long cushion was waddling toward them.

As this curiosity reached the front of the stage, the hum got louder when an indentation appeared from within near the top of the costume. There was a circular movement and then a small flap dropped down, revealing a man's face. Opaque blue glasses with round lenses the size of half dollars obscured his eyes, and putty distorted the shape of his cheeks.

Arms suddenly poked out from the tight elastic holes on either side, first reaching out high then slowly settling down, and the crowd ended its incantation by breathing out, "Modesty."

The face smiled and said, "Attention, mall shoppers. There's a sale on your likeness today. Over in electronics, that video of you smoking a cigarette at a backyard barbecue will result in your health care premiums being raised by fifteen percent. We also have some nice specials over in cosmetics on Forgiveness Cream—rub it into your pores and wipe that guilt away."

"Amen!" the crowd sighed.

"Yes, my children. You bear a great burden that comes from both ends of the hourglass. Deeds once lost to the past are unearthed and presented, not as conversation pieces or cautionary tales, but as evidence against you. And that which you do tomorrow shall give rise to new chains…"

Morgan stepped away from the railing and passed through the mingled smells drifting out from the cuisine court on his way to the escalator. He'd heard plenty of sermons by the Prescient One and other wise men since first arriving here two months ago—and right now he was desperate to find someone.

He passed a small photo booth that had been converted to accommodate hasty confessions, and which afterward printed out a laminated hologram stamped with the words, "Thank you for owning up to your sins!" Noticing legs under the curtain, Morgan surreptitiously peeked inside but saw that it was not his man. He walked on.

A group of tourists from Scandinavia was browsing outside a small storefront with Tribal American mannequins in the display. Souvenir t-shirts and mugs were neatly arranged at their feet next to a fake log fire. Rather than enter, the tourists turned their attention to a nearby open space where a middle-aged man was making an elaborate show of supplication at the base of a dark chrome cube. He waved a piece of paper toward its left side, and when this sheet was suddenly accepted and sucked in, he made a praying motion before crawling away.

Morgan rode the escalator down to the second floor and glanced into The Zap, where lines of white and black people stood on opposite sides of the store. He saw a white woman bow, then a black woman grazed her shoulder with an electronic flyswatter. The white woman twitched briefly, then bowed again and withdrew.

Morgan walked into the Tears anchor chapel. A greeter stepped forward and smiled.

"Good afternoon, novice," she said. "Are you making amends?"

"Not today, sister," he said. "I need to find someone else who's already atoning."

"I see. But may I remind you that all of the redressing rooms are private?"

"Yes, um, but my fellow apprentice requested that I help him remove a nagging burden from his conscience."

"Very well. Have a modest day…"

Morgan made his way down a long walkway toward the central redressing rooms. To the left he saw a large group of pilgrims who had laid a red felt tapestry on the floor which said: Third Indiana Penance Choir. Its forty members, dressed in matching black

Quaker suits with an embroidered Modidas logo on the left breast, were kneeling and weeping quietly.

He reached an area where two long rows of small doors faced each other. There was a line of people waiting at each end, and whenever someone exited one of the booths, an usher would scan the next guest's ticket and escort them in.

Morgan bypassed the line and headed directly to the stalls. A male usher caught up to him and said gently, "Sir, I'll need you to take a place in line."

"I'm not here to confess. My cloister-mate is having an atonement crisis. Stuck in 1756—please, can I help clear the blockage?"

"This is highly unusual, but if he's trapped…"

"Terribly. He's been working through this DE for weeks in our group therapy."

"Then of course…"

"Mod bless you!"

Morgan approached a door in the middle section and knocked gently. It cracked open and he could hear the hiss of a white noise machine inside. A bald man in a shimmering blue robe somewhat more ornate than Morgan's poked his head out from down below.

"What are you doing in here?" Morgan said, speaking as quietly as possible and suppressing the urge to scream. "We were supposed to meet by the cuisine court!"

"I know, brother," the bald man said. "I just got scared. Had to come back to my safe space, old lucky number 28. The thing is, he's built up such an important following here at the Mall—I don't see how he could be convinced to step away to help you."

Morgan opened the stall door wider and stuck his head inside, talking down to the other man who remained on his knees. "You let me worry about that.

Just follow through on your end and get me that meeting."

"Okay, okay. One hour. Down by the entrance to Victim's Secret."

"Finish your groveling and I'll see you there."

Morgan stormed out past the dozens of people standing in line, the tassels of his robe swinging back and forth with each rapid step. Two months of his life spent trying to blend in with these lunatics, and now his main contact was losing his nerve. Looking back, the antics he'd seen at the debtors' prison were an amateur display of contrition compared to what went on here, where spectacles worthy of a sports league's championship week took place on the hour.

Although it was initially churches and later HRA-inspired organizations that took advantage of the collapsed commercial real estate market by repurposing abandoned shopping malls across the country, the Mall of Absolution now set the gold standard for community spirituality in a guilt-ridden, post-work, post-functional society.

Here at the former Mall of America in Minnesota, an enigmatic figure called the Prescient One had turned its hauntingly empty corridors into a veritable Mecca for people seeking deeper meaning while they honored the nation's commitment to Reparations. These visitors believed that the formalities of wealth transfer and jobs training could only achieve so much, instead turning to the mystical realm of prayer to manifest lasting change. At their fingertips was a diverse offering of spiritual services, as well as historical tours, interracial healing sessions, VR past-life regressions in float tanks, gift shops, pan-civilizational dining, lectures by visiting scholars, and even a wedding chapel.

The Mall had also attracted seekers who felt that the

world, despite all the exciting changes and scientific breakthroughs, was actually collapsing in on them. Overwhelmed and desperate for asylum, they had entered its cavernous walkways not merely as guests but intending to make their lives here in simplicity. In response to their need, this destination-mall quickly morphed into a twenty-first-century castle complex outfitted with living quarters, a school, daycare, and rooftop gardens.

Three months ago, when the Haggerstons had first arrived in the Winnebago of fugitives at the resistance's Upstate New York compound, they underwent a strenuous few weeks of basic tactical training, learning about the nature of the mission, and ultimately specialized instruction for their upcoming assignments.

James and Ed were sent to canvass shanty tent cities to recruit homeless military veterans who still had enough fire in their bellies to fight for the America that existed in their minds. Gary had gone with Brick and a team of six other men in top physical shape to infiltrate a handful of HRA facilities, where they planned to install covert surveillance equipment.

And Morgan, having shown an ability to adapt to any number of pressure situations, was embedded with ten other underground operatives pretending to be recent converts to Modestianity who, in taking their initial vows, would live and work for two years at the Mall of Absolution. Their goal was to gain an audience with this reclusive Prescient One, a man rumored to have been one of the original designers of MARVIN's mainframe, but who'd had some sort of a breakdown and left the HRA shortly after launch.

He was said to have renounced all worldly possessions, refused to work on computers anymore, and some months later emerged from seclusion wearing a rectangular suit that looked like a blue ice cream sandwich. He began delivering inspirational, heartfelt, non-hypocritical sermons which encouraged people to be humble and forgiving, as well as advising discretion when facing the future.

Because the resistance believed that a strict repeal of the HRA would actually harm the nation, they sought someone with deep wisdom to lead a compassionate transition out of the program. The Prescient One's journey of disillusionment and awakening seemed to have prepared him to fill that role.

Further, his obsession with modesty had also resonated with other grassroots groups that accused the HRA of extending the reach of centralized surveillance so far that the legal concept of "prior restraint" was now actually bleeding over into people's daily lives. Citizens found themselves paralyzed into inaction as they asked themselves, "Is what I'm doing being recorded? How will it come back to haunt me?"

These various factions—unaffiliated but finding common ground within the bigger picture—saw a kind of genius in the Prescient One's eccentric variation of the full-body burqa, and felt it was urgent for the country to "have that conversation" before the noose of nosiness irrevocably tightened in a dreadful trinity of paranoia, blackmail, and humiliation.

Morgan was *this close* to finally presenting their case to the Prescient One—if only his contact could find some backbone while uttering Hail Modys from a prayer bench inside a converted changing room.

In the meantime, he needed to find a quiet place to compose his thoughts before this all-important meeting. The living quarters were out of the question because his fellow novitiates, while well-meaning, were always a little too talkative back in the cloisters.

Instead he made his way down the busy length of the mall to Mercies, another converted anchor store which, while as large as Tears, was devoted to the softer side of penance. Here, people struggling with the weight of their compounded guilt were afforded a reprieve from torment at one of several pleasantry stations.

There was a waterfall so loud that devotees could scream the worst hate speech imaginable without being overheard or recorded. Elsewhere, people put on VR headsets and entered a world where everyone's Debit Score was zero. Sometimes players refused to come back to real life or immediately got back in line, so this station was forced to impose a strict once-a-week policy in the interest of fairness and preventing addiction.

Morgan found a secluded atrium where pilgrims and residents alike sat on plush chairs, reflecting humbly under the benevolent gaze of enormous portraits of Sub-Saharan Jesus, Tribal Lincoln, and a waving Chinese train conductor.

He thought about his family, who he'd had no contact with in months, and said a little prayer while looking down at the floor. How had his life come to this moment? It seemed like only yesterday he was dropping his young daughter off at her first tee ball practice. But now he was a fugitive living incognito among people whose minds had been shattered by the psychotic philosophy that was snaking its way through the country.

Morgan had never claimed to be a saint, but also didn't think he was enough of a devil to warrant being shackled to a monthly bill that fluctuated every time MARVIN read the "D leaves." And though he was at a loss to pinpoint where things had begun to go wrong, he took heart in knowing that he was not just watching from the sidelines as events came to a head.

For people like himself who grew up in areas where the American Civil War was an intimate part of the soil, the conflict was seen as a dramatic chapter in the nation's history to be taught with respect and reverence, and without painting one side as villainous caricatures. It was a sweeping human tale full of great men and imperfect men, and common men dying tragically young in cornfields—impossibly far away from the larger narrative that said one thing in their day, and now sought to present a claim check on their lifestyle choices from out of an unearthed time capsule.

But the most palpable reason why Morgan detested the whole concept of Reparations had nothing to do with money. It was a memento most likely now sitting somewhere in an HRA evidence room: a tiny folding picture frame which had once sat on his grandfather's dresser, next to a little toy cannon and bottles of cologne. On one side was a photograph of a man with a beard wearing a dark military uniform. The other frame housed a man with a beard wearing a lighter military uniform.

Yes, blood relatives who had fought on opposite sides of the Civil War. A profound keepsake that revealed more about the complexities and mysterious paradox of life than words ever could. But in the eyes of the HRA and the pathological worldview it embodied, this heirloom was just one debt and one credit canceling each other out in two cells within a spreadsheet whose rows and columns cascaded like a cancer across a nation that was increasingly becoming so tentative and mistrustful as to not even dare to open its mouth.

The bald man was pacing nervously outside the entrance to Victim's Secret. Morgan approached and the man said, "You're sure you want to do this?"

"Now or never."

Two strongmen in satin robes opened the double doors and they walked in. The room was filled with dozens of fine blue drapes and veils, which they brushed past as they blindly went deeper inside, until coming upon an elevator. When they entered, Morgan saw that there were only two buttons—*1* and *B*—so he pressed *B* and felt the elevator descend.

Moments later the doors opened onto a sparsely lit room in which hundreds of long strips of blue cloth dangled from the ceiling, swaying gently in the cool air. As they crept slowly through this canopy of azure vines, the partially obscured figure of a man suddenly appeared a slight distance away.

"I'll be with you in one moment," he said.

Morgan turned to whisper something to the bald man but found that he had already disappeared, either into the maze of cloth or back into the elevator.

The Prescient One approached. Shed of his rectangular bodysuit and having removed the putty from his cheeks, he now wore loose-fitting silver satin shirt and pants, and from the top of his head dangled several pieces of wire that resembled blue licorice, each with a tiny rubber hand at the end which bobbed in front of his face. His eyes, no longer hidden by glasses, were nonetheless disguised by contact lenses whose speckled irises twinkled like stars in the night.

"Good evening, Mr. Walsh—or, should I say, Mr. Haggerston?"

"You're right," Morgan said. "That's my real name. How did you find me out?"

"Indeed," the Prescient One said, "you did quite well by not leaving much in the way of fingerprints. And your contact lenses, while not as effective as mine in concealing one's identity, didn't give you away either. You may take solace in knowing that you avoided detection by the HRA. But, myself feeling the need to defend this sanctuary against any potential threat, I take all of the obsessive precautions that a leader on his way out might."

"So what caught me?"

"Your toothbrush! And a hair in the shower. Oh, and—"

"I get it. How long have you known about me?"

"You *and* the others. You see, when I left the HRA —cracked up, as they say—it was my accursed foresight that drove me to establish this ark. And just as I understood the monster that we had given birth to —'He's a growing boy,' I used to warn the others about little MARVIN, 'it'll never be enough!'—so too I envisioned a time when someone on the outside would have the courage to fight back."

"We also have the strength," Morgan said, "but what we don't have is the vision to guide the nation through. We need *you* for that."

The Prescient One glided closer, though taking care to always keep some part of himself cloaked by the hanging fabric. "But *I* can't stop the HRA. Otherwise I would have done that before I lost my blue marbles."

"But you know it's about more than that. Look at how you've set up this place: on the surface it just looks like a community megachurch, but you added all these flavors around the theme of modesty. I had to think about that for a while. At first I assumed, probably like everyone else, that you were encouraging moral behavior to make better quality people, and maybe to reduce the odds of them committing crimes the HRA would punish.

"But after a while," Morgan continued, "I put it all together. You call this place an ark because you're waiting for a storm to pass—a deadly storm! All these precautions to cover people up, hide their identities in some way. You're obsessed with privacy, but I just don't know why."

"The phrase I use is 'private propriety.' We must defend it from the hungry eyes of MARVIN and his kind. To protect everyone here at the Mall, my technical team gives all security camera footage a 'dignity wipe' before it is passed along to the government—their mandate, of course.

"Consider this: if a corporation can be called amoral in its insatiable quest for profits, is the same not true for a supercomputer that craves new data? Especially now, when everything a person does has some sort of watermark attached to it, the MARVINs of this world will *never* run out of material to gather, organize, and judge. It is this shortsightedness baked into the HRA that will cause mankind to grind to a halt when his every move is put under such scrutiny."

"And that's exactly why we need you! You understand the danger and can express it so well."

"I've got my flock. They are free, they are protected here. And we are self-sufficient. When the system fails we will take our place as shepherds."

"After how many people have to die? There is a real resistance movement that has grown in just the past year—the situation now is so different from when you quit the HRA. If you ever left this cocoon maybe you'd see that it's time to strike!"

"Yes, yes," the Prescient One said with a wave, moving deeper into the blue thicket. "Everyone thinks their revolution is about to break out and win the day."

"Wait!" Morgan said. "You knew who I was, but do you know why I joined the movement?"

"I assume it has something to do with being penalized for destroying all of those antique documents."

"My wife and children were stolen from me. And if I don't turn myself in then I may never see them again. But let's say I go back and serve my time. What's stopping the HRA from grandfathering in new trumped-up charges to hang on my head later? Will I be sent back to prison again? This *will* all spin out of control, just like you said—and the only reason men like me haven't started a revolution yet is because we were told that you had the foresight to lead us over the rocky ground toward a better future. So don't you hide from us now!"

The Prescient One fiddled with one of the little blue hands bouncing in front of his face, then turned and disappeared behind a mass of blue cloth.

"If what you say is true, that an army is ready to take action, how exactly will my words be able to match your great might?"

"Because very soon we will bring your voice to the unsuspecting world."

7. SINS OF THE PAST

Several months after her dark night of the soul, Kate returned to work and a party was held in her honor. The coworkers who had visited her at home were especially happy, and everyone else was also pleased to have her back fighting the good fight. Within a week she was up to speed on all of the HRA's progress, and had personally met with the new staff hired to assist in facilitating overseas expansion. TJ had been promoted to head of his department, and Jan was the same as ever —a born leader walking confidently among the cubicles, boosting morale, offering constructive correction, and serving as feather-soother of last resort downstairs when necessary.

One afternoon a few weeks later, Jan stepped into Kate's office with a troubled expression on her face and quietly closed the door.

"Kate," she finally said, "I'm glad you're already sitting down. I just can't believe what I'm about to say."

"Okay… Has something gone wrong? Have *I* done something wrong?"

"Not you, per se. But close."

"Jan! Just tell me, what's going on?"

Jan pulled a folded piece of paper from her pocket and handed it to Kate.

"MARVIN spit this out on Sunday afternoon. I've been holding onto it trying to think of a gentle way to break the news, but there just isn't one. You came up as a DDM. Over twenty DEs."

Kate opened the printout and read the summons. It listed all of the Domination Events her ancestors had committed since the 1670s against the family of a man named Luis Ortega. At the bottom of the page it said they were required to appear on *DDM TV Live* in fourteen days.

She neatly refolded the paper and started straightening objects on her desk.

"Oh, Kate, I'm so sorry," Jan said. "If there was any way I could pull some strings to get you out of this, after all you've been through…"

"No, no," Kate replied, her face becoming serene. "It's alright. Equity means no special treatment. For anyone. Better for it to happen to me now after I've been sick, actually. I know so much more and can face the music… not with pride but… as much clarity as empathy."

The network couldn't resist advertising Kate's DDM as "the episode of the century," even though the show was only finishing its second season. The HRA also saw her appearance as a chance to cement its reputation as a truly accountable governmental organization, promoting it on the official website and with posters on field office walls.

As the show date approached, Kate began to feel that events were taking on a life of their own.

Coworkers were acting weird, her face was plastered all over the place, and the show's producers were calling and emailing at all hours of the day and night. Even debt protesters got in on the action by sending around memes that mocked "the absurdity of the century" and imploring the HRA to "stop throwing stones."

Kate even started to wonder how Chris would react if she was assigned somewhere far away. He had stood by her side like a rock during treatment, but facing the prospect of being separated for over six months out of the blue definitely had *her* in shock. Currently the DDM prize package only covered a Debtor's monthly bills, with no allocation for a temporary family move or visits, and in the big scheme of things Kate understood why. The HRA was in some ways like a Silicon Valley startup that sank billions of dollars for years before seeing a profit, so between infrastructure investment, day-to-day operation costs, and its worldwide expansion plans, brief separation of DDM families was considered a small sacrifice for people already on the hook for debts to society.

She'd first met Chris during her senior year of college. He was a guitar player in an aggressive, politically charged punk rock band that had some minor success touring around the Mid-Atlantic region, but in truth it was their upper-middle class sensibilities that had drawn them together. He once joked that they were both closet anarchists, happy to protest all day long before retreating to the comforts of a clean home not overrun by unshowered, transient activists.

During their early to mid-twenties, they made the semi-long-distance relationship work as she was often on the road advocating somewhere while he stayed local building a small web design business. Deep down, despite his now-defunct band's socially conscious lyrics, Chris only agreed with about half of the issues that Kate and her crowd were passionate about—but early on in their courtship he had been so captivated by the magical beauty that nature packs into a young woman, that there may have been no limit to the number of incomprehensible things she might say before he would give her up.

A private car picked them up on the evening of the show and drove them uptown to the network. Once they arrived, Kate was quickly whisked away to hair and makeup, then a PA took her to the mobile sound cart to be outfitted with a wireless microphone. After grabbing a bottle of water at craft service, she was instructed by the assistant director to be very careful not to mess up her makeup. This AD was a frantic little woman who would appear with a question or instruction every five minutes before disappearing to handle some other aspect of this pre-show symphony that she was conducting.

Kate could now hear the audience chanting in the background and an apprehensive glaze settled over her mind as she watched the crew hustling around. The atmosphere here seemed to have more of a bite than at that somewhat scripted *Tina* show she did six months ago, and in response she felt a burst of resentment toward the crowd. They knew nothing about her at all, so how dare they think of her as a sacrificial lamb?

To stifle this selfish impulse, she took heart in the knowledge that long term, this episode would only serve to give credence to the HRA's mission. *This is good press*, she reminded herself, *and I am the poster child—at least for this week*. Because as the show boasted, "no one can ever predict what shocking DDM connection MARVIN will make next," which would push her out of the headlines.

That encouraging last thought helped clear her mind. She took a careful sip of water and looked around. Crew members were still moving gear while in the background the audience was buzzing even more loudly. And over there was Chris talking to a cameraman—she perked up on tiptoes and gave him a wave. He smiled back then returned to his conversation.

Some of the backstage lights dimmed and the AD returned to lead Kate by the elbow to a curtain beside the stage. A man with a crew cut in khaki pants was gesticulating in front of the studio audience to get them riled up. And directly across from her on the other side of the stage behind a matching curtain, Kate could see Luis Ortega, whom she recognized from the promos.

Loud music and sound effects now blasted through the sound system—and into Kate's earbud—which prompted the crew to quickly clear off the stage. The main lights dimmed in some places while getting brighter in others, and finally a distinguished-looking man with sandy blond hair and artificially tanned face stepped onto the floor. The audience greeted him with loud applause which was accepted with a gracious wave before he tilted his head down, indicating a request for silence.

"Ladies and gentlemen, boys and girls. Watching around the world on great television networks and streaming all across the internet. I'm your host, Ryan Richards, and tonight I am honored to captain this historic episode of *DDM TV Live*.

"Our mission here on the show has always been to put a human face on the sometimes overwhelming project that the Historical Reparations Administration began just three years ago. Together we've seen centuries-old family feuds end in acts of goodwill, all documented here for posterity as a testament to the power of the human heart."

He struck a dramatic pose.

"And tonight, one of the HRA's very own walks into the belly of the beast to hear the roll call of her Bloodline Crimes, and dare to face her Direct Descendant Match. Together they will explore their long-intertwined fates, before mingling them one last time to gloriously end the cycle of victimization, and mend damaged fences once and for all!"

The lights went dark and all eyes turned to a large, elevated video screen behind the stage, which displayed a picture of Kate's face and several personal details.

"Mrs. Kathleen Donohugh," the host continued. "She goes by Kate. Born and raised in Arlington, Virginia. A longtime activist who worked tirelessly with so many others to make the HRA a reality, and where she now works at their large field office in Newark, New Jersey. Who would seemingly shine as a beacon for everything noble that the HRA advocates for—but *she* has a dark secret!"

The screen flashed to display the face of a young, light-skinned Latiz-American man wearing black-rimmed glasses.

"*Twenty-two* confirmed Domination Events perpetuated against this man's bloodline!"

The crowd erupted with howls and boos.

"Yes, it's true! And we here at *DDM TV* know what that means, so say it with me now…"

Everyone in the studio audience shouted in unison, "No one expects to pay for the sins of their fathers, but for you, that bill has come due!"

All the stage lights burst back on and Kate felt a nudge from behind so she walked out to meet Ryan Richards under a barrage of cheers and boos. She put on a gracious smile and shook the host's hand.

After the audience quieted down, he put his arm around her waist and said quietly, "Kate, you more than perhaps any other Debtor we've had on this program know where this is going. Do you want to say anything before we review the offenses spiraling savagely through every double-helix in your body?"

"Thank you, Ryan. I really want this to demonstrate to our critics that the HRA applies to *all* Americans. Not only do our employees truly believe in the mission, none of us try to hide behind sneaky exemptions or play favorites as often happens in big organizations."

"That's just wonderful to hear. Now, let's bring out your DDM. Please meet Mr. Luis Ortega!"

Cheers and applause broke out as the baby-faced young man in flat-brimmed baseball cap and skinny jeans ambled toward them. He gave the crowd a modest wave, then adjusted his glasses after shaking hands with the host.

"My goodness, Mr. Ortega, everybody!"

The audience worked up to a frenzy as Richards danced around and gave him a playful high-five. Kate stood to the side and clapped her hands.

"Luis, Kate. Kate, Luis."

Richards pretended to officiate as the two shook hands.

"Now, just to confirm, you two have never met each other before this moment?"

"That's right," Kate said.

"Well, after this brief commercial break, Kate Donohugh and Luis Ortega will *very much* get acquainted. Stay tuned, folks!"

The giant video screen behind them flickered a gray interference pattern for two seconds before switching to a car commercial. Richards craned his neck back to the screen, then shrugged his shoulders at the assistant director who was running up to them.

"That was weird," the AD said. "Anyway, when we get back from break, Ryan and the announcer will go down the list of Kate's DEs. The crowd's gonna eat it up. Then the mobile MARVIN unit will pass assessment. Kate and Luis, each of you will get a minute to speak, then it's off to our second DDM pairing of the night. Sound good? Great! Looks like we're back in thirty. Hold, smile, here we go…"

In the next segment, a baritone announcer rattled off a laundry list of crimes committed by Kate's ancestors, from the petty—livestock thefts and ethnic slurs—building up to various assaults, one rape, and finally a war crime that took place somewhere on the nebulous Texas-Mexico border in 1847. The audience was livid, practically frothing at the mouth, and getting restless for the cathartic payoff soon to come.

Several times Kate put a hand on her heart and mouthed "I'm sorry," and at other moments her eyes closed as she deeply felt eons of shame purge from her soul in this cleansing fire. Meanwhile Luis toyed with the zipper pull tab of his hoodie and shuffled his weight back and forth between feet.

After all of the DEs had been announced, the lights dimmed except for a center spotlight. Richards put his arms around them both and said, "You'd think that after nearly one hundred episodes we'd be numb to history's foul deeds, but I'm pretty certain we can all say that this is *not* the case. In fact, we are appalled by what has transpired between your two bloodlines. But now—tonight—at last. Justice, healing, and yes… Reparayyy-shuuuuuuns!!!"

A staggering roar surged through the studio and into the TVs, computer monitors, and phone screens of one-hundred-twenty-five-million viewers around the world.

The lights came up and Richards walked over to a machine that resembled a photocopier from the past. He pressed a red button and the machine flashed and whizzed, then spat out a red-and-black striped envelope. The host took it in his hands and walked solemnly back to center stage.

Richards pulled a silver letter opener from his jacket pocket and whipped it in front of his face with a swordsman's flourish. The crowd gasped as he proceeded to slit open the envelope with tantalizing care, then eased out a gold-rimmed card from within.

"Kathleen Donohugh," he said, "beloved HRA supervisor and guiding light of national atonement. You are hereby remanded to serve eight months at the Construction 4 Community build site in northeast Cleveland, where you and Luis Ortega will assemble low-income housing together. Standing side by side, your team will extinguish the flames of hate with every nail you hammer and each particleboard shelf you install."

In the stunned silence that followed, Richards began a slow clap which the audience built upon until the studio was pulsing with affirmation. He let them marinate in this deserved release for half a minute, then quieted them by lowering his outstretched arms. He stepped very close to Kate.

"Hi, Kate," he said softly.

"Hello, Ryan."

"Is there anything you'd like to say right now?"

She smiled, standing with hands clasped down by her waist.

"First, I want to say to you, Luis, what an honor it will be to go on this journey together as we bury history's hatchet."

Luis compressed his lips and gave a small nod.

"And what else?" Richards asked.

"I actually have a bit of a personal story to relate."

"*Oh?* Do tell."

"Well, everybody is aware of the public battles I fight each day working at the HRA. But what you don't know is that this past summer I went through a very personal struggle that taught me just how much work remains for us all.

"You see, I've just fought a battle against breast cancer. And what happened was that when I found myself betrayed by organs historically associated with what we call being a woman, I also felt my heart break for the people born into bodies that don't align with who or what is in their souls. Then I thought about all the other people in the world suffering from disease— be they cis, non-cis, trans, or straight—and I mourned for their losses as well.

"But the hardest truth I had to face was this: for all I suffered, the main reason I'm alive today is because I'm privileged in so many ways—my family, my education, my access to healthcare, and yes, my being *white*."

"Kate, that is a heartbreaking story no matter how you look at it. Just what do you propose?"

"We might have to expand the HRA's scope. Or create entirely *new* administrations tasked with meeting the needs of people who are oppressed in these other ways. Think about it—beyond the pain that came to my mind, what else must we heal? I know that the size of this potential project is enormous, but the main takeaway is that suffering exists now which lies beyond the reach of Historical Reparations, and I'll be damned if we let that need go unmet just because it was once in our collective blind spot."

Ryan Richards closed his eyes and joined his hands as if to pray. Seconds passed. Finally he said, "This is profound beyond anything we have ever gone through together here on *DDM TV*. Just now a Debtor transcended the bounds of our mission and placed a new path of responsibility before us."

Pivoting to Luis, he said with a grin, "I hate to throw all of this into *your* lap, young man, but wow! What do you say, buddy?"

Luis licked his lips and adjusted the brim of his hat, then looked around with wide, blinking eyes.

"It's pretty overwhelming, actually," he said. "My life's good right now, you know. I'm going to school in LA for electrical engineering, um, so I don't know. How's this trip to Cleveland gonna affect that?"

Just as Richards raised a finger and leaned in with a smirk, all the lights went dark and a loud buzz squawked from the sound system. The video screen above flickered a series of disjointed frames before all went quiet and a man wearing a shimmering silver Roman theater mask appeared, with bright blue dots emanating from inside the eyeholes.

"Violators and Victims," he said, "Debtors and Beneficiaries. We are the Sentinels of Jubilee. Today our moles seized control of the monstrous supercomputer called MARVIN that you beg for approval on history's box score. And I am here to declare that this misguided experiment known as the Historical Reparations Administration must come to an end."

The studio audience began to chatter while on the darkened stage below, Kate and Ryan Richards stood awkwardly in the screen's glow. She looked around and saw Luis fading away as he wandered behind a curtain.

"But we are not vindictive or bent on destruction," the masked man continued, the lights on his contacts pulsing and fading like an animated music player. "We acknowledge that the HRA was a somewhat noble effort, but this core idea of pressing pause on the future to replay old scenes is ultimately a futile endeavor.

"How can you discover the next great cure when you must constantly interrupt your concentration to pray to the god of Reparations, whose IV needle depletes all eruptions of creativity and passion? As if you could change that which can never be undone. No, it is through wisdom and teaching that you will achieve the goal of more building and less exploitation.

"But this is all a distraction from a bigger threat which looms. Consider this: if you are a Beneficiary, do you not think it possible that someday you could become a Debtor? The technology that MARVIN employs will only expand and zoom in more closely— no detail will be too small for the coming army of nanobot drones and microsensors that will monitor and upload every facet of life on Earth. You will all discover that history has indeed not ended, and your god MARVIN will pass excruciating judgment upon everyone in the sermon of his Holy Spreadsheet.

"And as each remote corner of Earth comes online, adding documents young and old, MARVIN will make deeper and deeper connections. There will be nothing you can hide, and nowhere to escape. The next frontier is not equity but total surveillance as humanity scurries in terror under the all-seeing eye of the Scrutiny State. *This* is your real enemy—not Reparations, or political parties, or even each other.

"Already this constricting existence is becoming too much to bear, always looking over your shoulder for sins committed by your ancestors in a different world —sometimes even centuries before the light bulb was invented! How can you protect *your* children and grandchildren against the acts you legally commit today but which will be reviewed, condemned, and punished tomorrow?

"This mechanism of our enslavement is already in place and that is why the HRA *must* change course before it is too late, before all trust between people is lost. We, the Sentinels of Jubilee, have drafted a plan which will remove the burden upon Debtors which has caused so much resentment, but we will not simply abandon Beneficiaries along the way. We must work together to establish codes which defend privacy and human dignity against the massive database which will surely be abused if not kept in check.

"Now, before I leave you, I have a message for this Ms. Donohugh. Kate, I sympathize deeply with anyone who faces a grave medical prognosis. But how can you think so little of yourself that in the moment of your deepest, most intimate personal sorrow, your instinct is to project it out onto anyone and everyone else? That is not compassion. Could it be that this self-effacing impulse is the same one that drives you to pick apart and micromanage every aspect of other people's lives? Is it possible that you have been brainwashed but don't even realize it? And most important of all, will the American people sit by while Kate and her millions of like-minded allies indoctrinate their own children?

"That is all for now. I will speak to you again when you are ready to take the next step. Good night."

The feed cut out and the screen switched to the *DDM TV Live* logo. The center spotlight came on and Kate saw Richards squirm as he tried to regain his composure—a producer was waving frantically at him from beside a nearby camera as the audience murmured in confusion.

"Uh, ladies and gentlemen," he said, wiping his forehead, "these impostors had *nothing* to do with our show and the important work we do. The culprits who dared to hack into our network will be caught and exposed for the cowards that they are."

He paused, put a hand to his ear, then said, "I've just been told by my producer that due to this security breach, it's in the interest of everyone's safety to end— if I may say—what had already been an unprecedented broadcast. Kate Donohugh and uh, well, I don't know where Luis has gone, but Kate, thank you for your dedicated service. We'll be checking in with you next week with an update from that housing project in Cleveland!"

The crowd gave tentative applause as Kate and Richards hugged then waved while the theme song played and show credits rolled on the screen above. As Kate began to pull away, the host whispered in her ear, "I think you're goddamned sexy. Come to my dressing room later and let's get our Reparations on."

Kate, still trying to hold a smile as the cameras circled them on stage, said, "What the hell! Is this all a big joke to you?"

"But you've got to help me, I have a sexi-medi-existential need. I'm a man that wants to feel trapped inside *your* body!"

Kate was revolted by the thick heat of his breath on her face and stumbled back, yanking away her wrist that he had taken hold of. She ran off the stage, saw Chris coming toward her, and they embraced. Tears began to stream down her cheeks and he tried to wipe them away.

"Hey, it's gonna be okay," he said tenderly. "Cleveland isn't so far away. What if they'd sent you to Phoenix?"

8. BRAINWASHED?

Immediately following the masked man's chilling declaration, HRA field offices nationwide were bombarded with phone calls, video messages, and visits from Beneficiaries terrified that they would stop receiving their deposits, as well as from Debtors eager to find out if their liability would be reduced or canceled. At the same time, Luis Ortega was nowhere to be found, and in light of the chaos at work, Kate was permitted to help out until he was located.

MARVIN was put into a protective stasis while techs scoured the millions of lines of code for any malware the hackers may have embedded. FBI security experts were brought in to help identify the moles who had infiltrated the HRA by posing as idealistic and trustworthy change agents, but were in fact bent on sabotage. The biggest challenge was that in addition to the core group of fifty thousand full-time staff, there were another eighty thousand contractors, part-timers, janitors, and volunteers to evaluate. It could take months to get an accurate picture of how compromised the HRA was. Meanwhile no one knew what the Sentinels of Jubilee intended to do next, or when.

The mood in the Donohugh household was subdued but anxious during these first days following Kate's appearance on *DDM TV Live*. Every time her phone beeped or rang it could mean that Luis Ortega had been found, and that she and Chris would then be separated for weeks or months.

After the third frantic day down at the field office, Kate came home with a case of red wine and declared that she was going to turn off her phone and force herself to relax. But even after two glasses, Chris noticed that she was still on edge and asked if something else was on her mind besides work.

"Who do you think the masked man was?" she said.

"Like, how did he end up as the mouthpiece for a group of hackers who claim they're saving the world, but he's still too afraid to show his face?"

"Sort of. I want to know what he was doing five or ten years ago. What drove him to hate the HRA so much?"

"Probably a Cauc," Chris said. "Start there."

"Obviously! But what else? How old is he?"

"I'd say late thirties to early fifties."

"Okay. But *who* is he? Seems to know a lot about tech and where it's going."

Chris took a sip from his wine glass.

"Truth is, some of what he said made a lot of sense. There is potential for abuse in the wrong hands, or worse, just losing control of it. MARVIN could be used to take cyberstalking to an insanely sophisticated level."

"But what are the wrong hands? Big scary government?"

"And corporations."

"But not you?"

"I'm a small fry. There's only so much reach an indie company like mine could have. I'm not one of these sexy startups that get huge investment capital every five years. I can't even imagine being able to do whatever I wanted with billions of dollars, then down the road just get more money because I'm big, or by telling the first investors they'll never get paid back unless they bail me out."

"But you chose to stay small. You could have found partners or approached banks for some loans, but I know you like the freedom of working from home."

"Yeah, but beyond that my life isn't very glamorous: no paid benefits, no fully stocked break room. Plus I have to deal with all the permits and fees, just like any other business. Look, I know corporations are evil and someone needs to keep an eye on them, but sometimes I just wish people who wrote policy actually did some for-profit work in the trenches. Then they'd see how hard it is to conjure up money from nothing, even without all the hoops they make us jump through."

Kate had perked up. "Which touches on another big problem. How many people of color never even find out what steps you have to take to go about starting a business?"

"Babe, just because I'm white and own a business, I still have to go out there and impress potential clients. They only care if I can get the job done for the right price, not my skin color. I'm sorry, but money talks!"

"No, there's so much more going on than just money. Countless Beneficiaries are never considered for those gigs because they're ten or fifteen years behind you in so many areas of life. What I—and the HRA—am trying to do is crack the code on how to get them up to parity with you."

"When did *I* become the official standard? There are designers, many from India—your next stop, by the way—almost half my age who have way better skills than me. And it's not like with my past client list I can just waltz in and land a big corporate contract. Don't hate me but, if you think the HRA needs to expand, why not go all the way and put *me* on the inside track with the big boys?"

"This is getting crazy. You could have gone in that direction years ago."

"I'm just saying, if you want to set some goals for helping people, then fine. But you can't pick a random person—me—and say that all Beneficiaries need to reach his level of X, Y, or Z."

Kate walked over to the curtain and looked out into the street. "What do you think he meant when he said millions of us had been brainwashed?"

"Man, this guy really got to you. I—and the dogs—am just glad you haven't been shipped out to Cleveland."

"Me too. But it *would* have been such a valuable experience…"

"Wait! Maybe that's it right there. What that guy with the mask meant. I'm your husband, you're supposed to want to be with me. These symbolic group activities—I just don't get it."

"So I have to stay by your side like some woman of the past who had no rights?"

"Kate, that is such a mental leap."

"But it's not taking a leap to side with the freak in the mask who thinks I, your darling wife, was indoctrinated without even knowing it?"

Chris put his hands up. "Let's pick it apart then, rationally."

"Okay, how?"

"Imagine a woman," he said, "who's the exact opposite of you. Let's call her Kimberly. How is she different? Is she evil?"

"Well... She doesn't advocate for others. She doesn't fight for human rights. She doesn't consider that her every action has an expanding butterfly effect on the world. Instead she just does whatever she feels like."

"Interesting. So she doesn't rob banks or shoot people?"

"No."

"Doesn't go to cross burnings?"

"No."

"Just works a normal job, watches movies, vidchats with her friends, and *maybe* has an extra scoop of mint ice cream in secret after her husband goes to bed?"

"Hey! I thought you said we were opposites!"

"I know, I was kidding," Chris said with a smile. "But maybe not completely. Maybe this Kimberly lives a quiet, decent life not much different from yours."

"Yeah, but she's still enjoying the advantages of her privilege even if she doesn't know it."

"Okay, right there—where did *that* idea come from? You didn't think of it yourself and Kimberly certainly doesn't believe it."

"I don't know," Kate said, moving away from the window. "I'd have to think back. Sometime during middle school, maybe? Possibly at an assembly or in history class."

"Since when was the point of school to tell students how they benefited from the events being taught? I mean, pretty much everyone's lives have been improved by the invention of the wheel, right? But some people actually get run over by them and die, and there might be a remote tribe somewhere that still hasn't made first contact with the outside world. Do we somehow have to make it up to all of them?"

"Chris! Do you realize what you're saying right now and how that makes me feel?"

"You said you wanted to know if you'd been brainwashed. I'm just playing along and asking the tough questions."

"So you're saying it'd be better to live like Kimberly and just let the Beneficiaries fend for themselves for another five hundred years?"

"Did you not hear what that guy in the mask said? MARVIN may be programmed back to 1492 right now, but it's not going to stay that way forever. When did the Moors invade Spain? Way before Columbus! Are some Afrigo-Americans going to have to pay Reparations to descendants of The Conquistadors, who then just pass it right along to Tribal Americans?"

"Oh my god!" Kate screamed. "What kind of connection is that?"

Chris took a deep breath and spoke deliberately.

"I don't think any of you understand the can of worms you've opened with this. After you 'franchise' out to other former colonies and the homelands of their white invaders, it's not just going to stop there. I'll give the hacker this: he understands that the computers are going to reach not just *out* but *back*. Until every country is at each other's throats trying to get repaid for every war, every broken treaty, every sunken ship…"

Kate was in shock. She sat down against the base of the couch and pulled up her knees. Of all the people she had done intellectual battle with, she never expected that Chris would be the one to say the worst things of all.

"So the HRA has been a big mistake? You think I've wasted half my life building something that's going to stop the world? I'm just… speechless. How long have you been thinking all this?"

"Only during the last couple days since the show, really."

"And what did you think before?"

"Katie, I've always supported whatever it was you were doing. If you were happy, then that would help make *us* work."

"My god. All this time. You never actually cared about the Victims."

"I care about you. I hope you can say that about me."

Kate stood up and walked back to the window. Some homeless people were pushing carts down the sidewalk. She knew that she should give Chris an answer but she also wanted to see if there was an extra blanket in the hall closet she could take down to help keep them warm.

Maddie, one of the Corgis, nuzzled at her feet. She squatted down and rubbed its ears, then said, "And I wuv you!" She froze and looked over at Chris, whose jaw had dropped.

"I'm going to put an asterisk beside this conversation," he said. "Everyone's stressed out right now. But I think I'll sleep in my office tonight." He got up and went into the bathroom.

Kate sat down next to the dog and stroked its neck absently.

Later that night, alone in bed while the dogs slept on the floor nearby, she couldn't stop thinking about how she'd said that she might have been brainwashed at school. It was so strange, because all of her memories from elementary school through high school graduation were of a positive place that encouraged cooperation and had no tolerance for ugly words, ignorance, or fights.

Yet somehow at college she didn't gravitate to the Greek party scene, or even a casual volunteer club, but instead fell in with righteously angry left-wing activists. She had been so happy all of her life up until they bombarded her with "the truth," and the next thing Kate knew she was their newest recruit, complete with green-dyed short hair and a nose ring. And though tempted, she could never bring herself to get a tattoo like so many of the others—because her "bourgeois soul refused to die," according to one of several regrettable dating choices she'd made during the reckless early phase that, in time, achieved balance with her former self.

Indeed, it was this coming into her own that had set the direction for the rest of Kate's life, and not the marketing degree she earned from the college. Maybe somewhere her doppelganger Kimberly had a shelf lined with advertising industry awards, but Kate was actually changing the world. And she didn't feel like a Manchurian Advocate for doing it, either!

But tonight, here in bed by herself, these affirming thoughts could not help her fall asleep. She pictured Chris scrunched up on that tiny sofa in his office. She got up and walked over to him, cramming herself up against his body under the thin blanket. She nuzzled him on the cheek.

"I looked up what 'jubilee' means," he said drowsily. "In ancient times, kings would forgive all the debts and everybody started fresh again."

"I owe you an apology, Mr. Donohugh," she said softly. "And I might know of a way to get you to forgive *my* debt..."

9. UNDER FIRE

NIFTY MINUTES – SEASON 61, EPISODE 3 –
"HRA UNDER FIRE"

BEGIN SHOW TRANSCRIPT

Cheryl Li: Three years ago, the Historical Reparations Administration launched in the United States to great fanfare. It is an ambitious project which aims to right the wrongs of history and level the playing field after centuries of inequality. While any government agency can expect its share of challenges and negative press, in recent weeks two major stories have broken to cast a shadow of doubt across the young program that is so filled with hope. Our Howard Parnell reports.

Howard Parnell: Good evening, I'm Howard Parnell for *Nifty Minutes*. In this segment we will investigate why the HRA finds itself under fire from both sides of the spreadsheet, as well as explore what can be done to right the ship.

(voice-over) Our story begins in the city of Newark,

New Jersey. It is one of many poor, predominantly Afrigro-American cities that the HRA targeted as a beachhead in its War for Equity. But as we will see, residents on the ground say that nearly three years in, life here has not gotten much better.

(video: A black teenager moves to the beat of hip-hop in a vacant city street at night.)

Singer: Drones fly by, money flow in. Reparations, why? Because we're victims. You got the document scan, in MARVIN we trust, but the streets still bleed, so where we at?

Parnell (voice-over): Meet fifteen-year-old Clyde Jenkins, aka DJ Clydoscope. He lives at home with his mother, has never held a real job, and admits to having stolen a number of the HRA mini-drones which patrol the city. But it's his surprise indie hit single "Fly So High," whose lyrics paint a not-so-rosy picture about the realities of life for HRA Beneficiaries, which has struck a deep chord nationwide among people dissatisfied with the program. Some are even calling Clyde the voice of the half-decade in light of this "DJ versus Goliath" phenomenon.

(on camera) Two months ago you were a complete unknown. Now your song is the hit of the year. What do you think about all that's happened?

Clyde Jenkins: It's really crazy. Like, I knew it was a good track, but I just hoped enough people would feel it to inspire me to write more.

Parnell: You didn't expect to be famous, just like that?

Jenkins: No! I mean, you dream but... how many people's dreams come true, especially where I'm from?

Parnell: What motivated you to write the song?

Jenkins: People still getting robbed, killed. So many cameras out there now, guess the HRA can see all they money being spent on drugs and all the rest.

Parnell: Does the song's popularity among other Beneficiaries encourage you in thinking that the HRA will respond by making changes?

Jenkins: Hey, I only put out the message. It's not in my hands anymore.

Parnell: Do you ever just pinch yourself and ask, "Is this even real?"

Jenkins: Well, it feels weird having all these fans, you know. Maybe in the hood, I get it. But why would someone in like, Japan, get down with my message?

Parnell (voice-over): But resonate he has. One music critic says, "The effortless turn from aggressively rapped lyrics about street life into a soulfully crooned chorus—which soars with lightness and spirituality—shows me exactly why this young man has taken the world by storm." Even the legendary rapper MC Ergo No Mic weighed in, saying, "He's like the new Tupac. Young, fierce. Sees how things are, tells it like it is. And too young to know better than to hold back. Respect!"

One friend Clyde doesn't have? The HRA. The fact that he used stolen government property to film a no-budget video which undermines the administration's multi-million-dollar marketing campaign, isn't sitting well with management—and now their lawyers are out to seize his earnings. But DJ Clydoscope takes it all in stride.

Jenkins: I'd say it's typical, you know. Kids be out there smashing them drones the whole time. HRA could've stopped us if they wanted to. But before, I was just a poor helpless kid—a *Beneficiary*—I *needed* their help. Now that I got a voice of my own, HRA come collecting for services rendered real quick!

Parnell (voice-over): Elena Forsyth, an HRA

spokeshuman, disagrees with the harsh assessment Mr. Jenkins makes, both in his interview and in the song.

Elena Forsyth: None of us have any animosity toward him. In fact, he's an empowered young person of pigment expressing himself. I'd like to think that the HRA gave him a boost, even if he doesn't see it that way.

Parnell: But what about the allegations of Beneficiaries gaming the system like the welfare abusers of old, with no oversight, and the seeming anarchy on the streets after sunset in these poor neighborhoods?

Forsyth: Some areas are worse than others. Newark historically has had a high crime rate. I don't think one song written by someone living in such a challenging place should be considered a referendum on the whole program.

Parnell: Then how do you explain the fact that it's getting airplay all over the country? There have been over eleven million downloads, countless audio streams, plus PerformTube reports sixty-five-million views. That's unprecedented for an unknown artist— something about his message *is* resonating with people from coast to coast.

Forsyth: You know, Howard, I watched the video several times—

Parnell: Oh, really?

Forsyth: Yes, we've all seen it—and it *is* a catchy tune—but my takeaway is the inspiring message of hope it sends. When you see the sun coming up over the city, the aerial ballet of the synchronized drones swirling above—

Parnell: Drones stolen from your organization, which is now threatening to slap Mr. Jenkins with legal action...

Forsyth: No one wants to take this kid to court—

Parnell: As if you haven't gotten enough bad press already...

Forsyth: Exactly. What we at the HRA would all like to do is get back to work, and we hope that this one-hit-wonder doesn't discourage people or make them impatient. We've made great strides, but admittedly there's still a lot of work to do out there.

Parnell (voice-over): But that's not all the HRA has to worry about. A much more formidable group calling itself the Sentinels of Jubilee hacked into the administration's flagship show, *DDM TV Live*, just days before this episode was scheduled to air. That "October Surprise" exposed serious vulnerabilities in the HRA's computer network which houses data on every American citizen, as well as gave troubling confirmation that disgruntled Debtors are preparing to fight back. While their plans—and masked leader— remain somewhat cryptic, the HRA has been put on notice.

I spoke with Molly Kleiner of the Thinkings Institution in our nation's capital. (on camera) Molly, what do you believe is going on out there?

Molly Kleiner: I think any time you try to roll out a large new program, people want to see immediate results. You're under a lot of scrutiny to show what good all that money is doing.

Parnell: Scrutiny. That's the same word used by the masked hacker on *DDM TV Live* the other night. Any thoughts on his fears that the technology could spin out of control?

Kleiner: Anyone who thinks the surveillance network is something new needs a brief lesson in recent history. The NSA and CIA had long been spying on American citizens by the time the Neocons took surveillance to the next level when they created the Department of Homeland Security. Not only that, people have voluntarily posted their whole lives on social media sites for years. But now that the left-wing activists are in charge, it's finally a problem? I find such fearful criticisms ironic because the HRA is actually using this data to implement policy in a forthright manner.

Parnell: But they're looking back into hundreds of years' worth of information, not merely at people alive today.

Kleiner: It is no crime to execute laws by making use of a utility that was built before your tenure. Even if people don't like what the Dramacrats are doing to the place, they didn't build it—it's been here for quite a while.

Parnell: What would you say to those people who look at HRA failures—their word—failures like Newark, and say, "Whoa, whoa. They want to expand and one day do an accounting of the British East India Company while there are serious problems here at home?" Is the beta test maybe not over yet?

Kleiner: The program's vast scope almost guarantees that it will take many years to complete. They can't just leave Victims waiting worldwide. Besides, the system's design is sound—they just need to plug it in overseas and adapt as they go.

Parnell: Before I let *you* go, what are your thoughts on the "Fly So High" phenomenon?

Kleiner: However crude, I think the song carries an important message that the HRA should heed. Because look, if we're asking the nation to be accountable for its history, then surely the administration needs to honor that philosophy itself.

Parnell (voice-over): One interesting player in this

whole drama is Nolan Simmons. A US Army veteran who's currently embedded deep within the mean streets, he also directed the "Fly So High" music video. And he's got a lot to say.

Nolan Simmons: We've got all these people who lack the life skills to keep it together, let alone compete. They've been on the government dole for decades, so giving them more money under a new name—Reparations, this time—it isn't going to help. And now you're really making white people angry! Before, they just had to pay taxes, but now someone's pointing a finger at them.

Parnell: So what is the HRA doing wrong, in your opinion?

Simmons: It's a bunch of people with master's degrees coming in and using us as guinea pigs. And when their brilliant ideas fail, there's no negative consequences for their careers or even taking a moment to ask, "Hey, what did we do wrong?" It's just a tragedy that the HRA is run by so many fools.

Parnell: Why do you call them "fools"?

Simmons: Because they think they're social workers. But their minds work like anthropologists or missionaries trying to "save the natives." They're so out of touch from our experience. They've never suffered, they've never been desperate—so the ideas that work in their world just won't take down here.

Parnell: Okay. If the HRA approached you tomorrow and said you were in charge, what would you propose?

Simmons: I'm not saying that we need to be left to our own devices, but there has to be some sort of middle ground between this going back and forth. Where one year there's more law enforcement presence, but the next year, a cop is nowhere to be found. I'm not blaming anyone, but the fact is that real bad guys fill that void.

Now, as for solutions. From my own life experience, it was the discipline of the military that made me a functional person—the consistent rules, enforcement, and consequences. So maybe we need small military academies in these poor cities—at least something like how private schools are set up—to help turn these little gang militias into an Inner City Corps of Leaders who will rebuild and protect their own neighborhoods. And no more centralized decrees! Let the communities save themselves by becoming more self-sufficient, just like the HRA wants.

Parnell: What do you say to people who would call you a hypocrite? Here you are, a former US government employee, and yet you filmed this music video with stolen HRA property.

Simmons: You know, I get it. But I help keep the corner of my hood safer, keep some of these guys out of real trouble by teaching them skills and responsibilities. I could've left town—my military experience would have opened doors for me to get a job in a safer area. But it's just like immigration: if all the smart, capable people leave to go to a nicer country, how's the old place ever gonna improve? We have got to stop the brain drain, and work to increase the pain drain!

Parnell: Well said. That actually sounds like it could be one of Clyde's lyrics.

Simmons: I'm glad you mentioned him. Because, you know, I'm taking a real risk putting my face on this show. But I think the message in his song is so important, and somehow we have this amazing opportunity to speak to the rest of the country—I owe it to the people who don't have a voice.

Parnell (in studio): Right now the HRA is reeling from a one-two punch of bad press and "technical difficulties" just weeks before the president's re-election bid. We'll learn in the coming days how well the program responds, and if Rebellican challenger Victor Dominguez—who so far has said very little about the HRA—decides to pounce. For *Nifty Minutes*, I'm Howard Parnell, giving young DJ Clydoscope the last word.

Jenkins (singing): But this ain't me, eye in the sky knows, this ain't how things supposed to be. So for all we can see, and all we can be. We got to fly, fly so high, and find a way, way outta here… alive.

END SHOW TRANSCRIPT

10. THE FUGITIVE

At a gas station along one of South Dakota's lonely highways, an infrared camera—serving as part of the national Predator Predator network, which scanned all vehicles passing through certain points on known human trafficking routes—logged the image of a person squeezed into a small crevice in the back of an old pickup truck.

A silent alarm was sent to both the FBI and the nearest police dispatch, and the truck was followed at a discreet distance by a drone paired with the camera mount. This unarmed drone sent encrypted night-vision video and GPS pings back to its charging base and out to nearby cell towers, which were then relayed to law enforcement with an impressively brief lag time.

Fifty miles west of the first sighting, near the outskirts of Rapid City, FBI agents swung into action staging a violent car crash scene involving three civilian vehicles, a fire truck, and two ambulances. Tow trucks lowered the smashed cars into place while crisis actors changed into torn clothing and applied makeup and fake blood. They, along with the paramedics, were all FBI agents trained for dangerous apprehensions such as this. The local police, whose cars were borrowed to make the scene look more realistic, were instructed to stand aside, and several agents who had put on police uniforms would make any direct contact with the vehicle of interest.

This elaborate ruse had sprung out of an Ambrosia Alert gone tragically wrong. A father who had abducted his two daughters from his ex-wife's home panicked after his car was suddenly surrounded by police on a highway. He swerved off the road near an overpass and the car plunged thirty feet into a river. It took two days to locate the bodies, and the nation mourned for a week.

Even the most stubborn FBI bureaucrats, not ones for changing agency policy in response to an exceptional circumstance, were now at least willing to consider less direct methods of engagement. Among several new concepts secretly being beta tested was the fake car crash ruse, and the bigwigs were anxious to see how tonight's exercise played out.

As a dozen FBI drones fanned out down the three miles leading up to the crash site, the original drone in pursuit was instructed to turn back and return to its charging station once it reached this perimeter. The central Predator Predator computer system notated a commendation for this camera/drone team pending the outcome of the chase.

Real civilian passenger vehicles began to line up and trickle through the modified traffic pattern, which had shifted over one lane so that eastbound cars drove on their right shoulder and westbound cars went down what would normally have been the wrong-way lane.

Because there were no convenient entry points

along this wilderness highway, the FBI was not able to pull any faux-civilian vehicles directly ahead of or behind the suspect's truck. They would have to rely on a quick converging strike to simultaneously disable the vehicle and immobilize the driver—the latter being a very delicate process because saving lives had to be weighed against the risk of pricey civil rights lawsuits.

The truck slowed down into the traffic jam a half mile behind the crash site, and night-vision cameras sent back the image of an older man with a mustache wearing a cowboy hat. As the line of cars slowly moved forward, agents that had dispersed along the roadside for the last quarter mile kept radio contact, some observing through night-vision binoculars, others through the optics of their sniper rifles. All reported that the driver seemed calm and had made no movements toward the truck's camper.

The scene of the staged crash was filled with flashing lights shooting out and crisscrossing in all directions. Cars rolling past could see two overturned vehicles, shattered glass sparkling in the cascade of lights, and paramedics tending to passengers on stretchers and applying bandages outside the open rear doors of the ambulances. Police officers carefully directed traffic around the debris field while firefighters kept a wary eye on the wreckage.

Suddenly a flashbang sent a blinding burst of white light in front of an older pickup truck. Bodies seemed to rise from the dead as accident victims leaped from their stretchers and converged upon the truck.

A loud crash as the driver's window was shattered, then a quick slice through the seat belt, and four incredibly strong arms wrenched him out through the window frame. He was hustled away to the side of the road and placed on his stomach, the cowboy hat falling away into the dust as his hands were cuffed.

A team leader threw open the back of the truck with his weapon drawn. Directly behind him at the ready were three armed agents, a paramedic, and a child psychologist of each traditional gender. Slowly, the leader moved toward a false cover and then pried it open with a crowbar.

Flashlights poured into the void and up sat a terrified young man in glasses. He was pulled out of the cubby and a blanket was immediately thrown over his body. The psychologists embraced him, one putting a teddy bear into his hands, and gave assurances that everything was going to be all right.

The young man was slowly led away to the nearest ambulance for an on-site examination to make sure he had no life-threatening injuries. The FBI tactical team was giving congratulations, but kept its distance out of respect for the severe trauma this victim had endured. Other agents had already loaded the driver into one of their vehicles to be interrogated later.

When the EMT determined that the young man was in good health, he picked up a tablet and said, "Now, young fellow, I'm just going to scan your eye so we can find out where your mommy and daddy are."

"No, no, please," the young man said, waving a hand in front of his face.

"Don't be shy now, mister. We need to know who you are, now don't we?"

"Please, I just want to go back to school…"

"And you most certainly will, tough guy. You've been such a trooper already. Just… Come on… Let me see…"

"Nooooo!"

The young man bolted away from the ambulance back toward the truck, but several of the wounded crisis actors were standing nearby and quickly surrounded him.

"Say," a woman with fake blood all over her face and arm said, "he looks just like that guy who disappeared from *DDM TV* the other day."

A man in fireperson's gear said, "My god, you're right! *It's Luis!*"

"We found him! We found him!"

The young man could not comprehend this scene of crashed cars, flashing emergency lights, buzzing drones, and the joy that finding him had put on the faces of people who had seemingly suffered horrendous injuries. He brought his hands up to his face and collapsed onto the ground as FBI agents danced in a circle around him.

As the last traces of the post-World War II boom receded like a river in a drought, the United States was uncertain about how to maintain its power and standard of living. The chaotic scramble that followed, playing out on both the macro and micro stages, characterized much of early twenty-first-century American life, and is now referred to as the Great Free-for-All.

A costly series of dubious wars exhausted the military. Systemic mortgage fraud devastated millions of people when the lies woven into the corrupt financial sector also collapsed. Rampant abuse of prescription medications and illicit drugs put nearly half the population into a dependent stupor. Government bailouts to the tune of trillions of dollars were crafted in secret and siphoned off with no oversight. The dying healthcare Ponzi scheme was replaced by a compulsory national program whose bill Congress was not even allowed to read before voting on. Countless foreigners crossed the southern border without paperwork and were allowed to stay in the country indefinitely. And seemingly every other young woman posed nude online or had a sex tape.

Morale and morality were both in the gutter when the rumblings of a more conservative attitude began to appear online, slowly percolating in an information war that culminated in 2016, when its shocking roar swept a protectionist political amateur into the White House. The Great Free-for-All is said to have officially ended early in 2021 when this president signed the pragmatic HOLA—Honoring Our Legacy as Americans—immigration bill into law.

In the interest of finally not looking the other way—cheap labor was simply no longer a valid excuse in a deindustrialized nation threatened by wandering jihadis and an increasingly automated workforce—both political parties made tremendous trade-offs in writing the legislation. No one wanted to risk the eternal political fallout of trying to round up and deport (what turned out to be) sixty-eight-million undocumented people from around the world who had entered illegally or overstayed a visa. This number did not even include their offspring born on US soil.

Jowls of indignation jiggled furiously during the historic late-night debates between career politicians who had sat idly by for decades, happily drinking mint juleps while American industry sank into a swamp of outsourcing and regulation due to their shortsightedness and blackmailable predilections. Young congresshumans begged them to consider how their grandchildren would actually live, rather than worry about what the biographers would say about them later.

In the end, the Rebellicans were willing to hold their noses and accept "Hopefully One Last Amnesty" if the Dramacrats promised not to unleash their army of civil rights attorneys when, as a condition of being granted citizenship, these immigrants were required to register for the National Biometric Identification Database—complete with fingerprinting, face and retinal scans, and submitting a DNA sample.

After the signing ceremony, the president wistfully suggested in a post to his skReacher account that the Supreme Court "just let this one go" so that America could keep moving forward. Cynical types believed that the Rebellican president had intentionally waited until winning a second term before biting the pragmatic bullet and passing amnesty, which might hand the Dramacrats power for years to come.

For the left-wing activists who had been stewing in their own juices since Inauguration Day 2017, this unexpected milestone proved to be a revelation that showed them a way forward. Instantly millions of people they had previously advocated for were now on the path to citizenship, and very likely to give their next presidential candidate enough votes to win the 2024 election in a landslide.

That the Rebellicans, under the auspices of creating a national voter ID system, would agree to support a citizen database, played right into the HRA activists' hands. First by collecting data that could be used to build comprehensive profiles of prospective Debtors and Beneficiaries, but also in helping to pave the way for an electronic currency which would transfer funds automatically. The days of hiding gold in grandma's mattress were finally coming to an end!

For the likes of Luis Ortega, who had been brought across the Mexican border as a baby and whose dreams were not nearly so lofty as the HRA founders', becoming officially legalized was an incredible weight off his shoulders. He would never have to fear returning home from school to find that his parents had been deported, and his aging grandfather was later permitted to come live with them in his final days.

He grew up near downtown Los Angeles, becoming an avid skateboarder and fan of the Dodgers baseball team. While not the best student in school, he spent a lot of his time working on old electronics which his father and uncle brought home as part of their scrap business. So in his senior year of high school he applied to some of the local community colleges, and when his DDM notice arrived from the HRA, Luis was already deep into his second semester of technology classes.

Luis and his family had never really been interested in what the Reparations program was about. While they did appreciate the modest monthly stipend, the Ortegas were still glowing in the wake of legalization and being able to make concrete plans for the future. Being called upon to appear on a national television show was a mortifying shock for the soft-spoken young man—his parents risked and sacrificed so much to give him the opportunities they'd never had, and all he wanted to do was make them proud.

The whole process of flying out to New York was a self-conscious nightmare he had just tried to endure. As a Beneficiary, Luis was considered the guest of honor and found himself showered with attention by the press and fans of the show. He hid in the hotel suite until absolutely required to come out and go to the studio for filming.

When he first saw the white woman who was his DDM standing across the stage, he didn't understand why the audience was so angry at her. Later, as her ancestors' crimes against his family were announced, all he could think about were his cousins Umberto and Carlo, who had been brutally murdered four years ago by cartel members down in Juarez, Mexico. No news station reported on their deaths—just a drop in the bucket, sadly—and the police never found their killers.

He couldn't see why he had to go to Cleveland with this woman he didn't even know, so when everybody got confused after the lights went out, his feet started walking of their own accord and took him off stage.

First he went to the dressing room to get his phone, but when one of the PAs got in his face and asked if he was supposed to be back on stage, he realized that these people weren't going to leave him alone. He told the PA that the AD said he could take a five-minute break, then quickly ran out of the building.

Having grown up in a big city, Luis wasn't intimidated by Manhattan despite its endless rows of towering buildings. He was relieved to be away from all that craziness inside and strolled a few blocks before calling his parents back home.

"Oh my god, Luis! Is that you?" his mother screamed.

"Yeah, it's me. I'm fine."

"But what happened? Where did you go?"

"I think someone maybe hacked into the show. I didn't want to be there anymore so I left."

"But they're going to be looking for you, *mi vida.* You have to go to Cleveland!"

"I don't wanna do that stupid stuff. I need to get home, get back to my classes."

"*Dios mio!* What are we gonna do?"

When an APB with Luis's face was broadcast nationwide, the family realized that he would be apprehended if he tried to use any form of commercial travel. His father made a few phone calls and put Luis in touch with a man named Etienne Galvez, a retired coyote from back in the Great Free-for-All days who went by the nickname El Perro. The Ortegas wired him two thousand dollars to smuggle Luis from New York back to California.

It was during the long, uncomfortable hours hidden inside the secret compartment of El Perro's truck that for the first time in his life, Luis truly and profoundly understood the dangerous journey that his parents had undertaken. He had been too young at the time to remember any of it, and now whispered an emotional prayer of thanks to God for everything he had.

When the flashbang outside the truck jerked him out of the semi-meditative state he'd developed to pass the hours, Luis thought they had gotten into an accident. He hoped everyone was okay, especially El Perro, otherwise he might be forgotten in this hiding place. The frantic sequence that followed—his "liberation" and the disturbing spectacle of bloody people dancing all around—was simply too much to take, and he fell to his knees before blacking out completely.

11. SCRUTINY

Five days after the hack, Kate was called in to an early morning meeting of trusted supervisors. Jan pulled her aside before they entered the conference room.

"Kate, I want you to know how glad we are to still have you here with us. Could you imagine being trapped on the outside, walking around in a tool belt while all this was going on? At nine o'clock there'll be another hundred people lined up downstairs freaking out because they think their next payment won't get deposited."

"I'll be there to give assurances. And more autographs…"

"Yeah, everyone's got something to say about you after that speech you gave! Anyway, just keep doing what you're doing. But stay inside the building and be sure to have security walk you out tonight. There's just too many people on edge and a couple fist fights have broken out in the parking lot."

"Feels like three years ago all over again, doesn't it?"

"Mm-hmm." Jan shook her head. "Except *we* had the momentum back then."

Kate and ten of her coworkers sat around a large table reviewing printouts as Jan led the conference call with one of the national directors.

"Hi, Peter," Jan said. "We're all here. What's the latest?"

"Good news and bad news," said the face on the large wall-mounted flat screen. "The good news is that the FBI has pinpointed the location of the rogue broadcast to within a two-mile radius in Wilmington, Delaware. Our techs and their strike team are coordinating a seize-and-shutdown raid as we speak."

"Okay! Get these guys before they cause any more panic."

"Exactly. But the bad news is that our code crawlers, after just a cursory analysis of twenty-four percent of MARVIN's software, have already detected —not any malware or viruses, per se—but suspicious footprints that suggest tampering in at least thirty-six HRA locations."

Jan looked down the table and waved to a South Korean-American man who was madly swiping and tapping on his tablet. "Tyler, any thoughts on this?"

"Yeah," he said, glancing up. "Peter, Tyler Cho from IT here. Is there any possibility that these red flags could have originated from a single source but were only placed in such a way as to make the hackers seem stronger than they really are? You know, to give them more leverage against us and public perception?"

Peter let out a long sigh. "Do I ever wish that were the case. It's possible. And we'll know a bit more as soon as we can get our team on the ground in Wilmington. But until then we're advising every field office to proceed under the assumption that they may have been compromised and that there could be a mole among them."

Everyone looked around the table at each other. Jan spoke up.

"Well, I can vouch for the people in this room, or else we've got a really big problem. Obviously, we won't say a word about this Wilmington situation until it plays out. Thanks for the update and trust, Peter."

Moments later about half of the cell phones around the table pinged at virtually the same time. People checked their screens, then looked over at Jan. She too had received a message and, after typing briefly into her phone, instructed the assistant who had run the conference call to bring up the link she had just sent him.

The picture on the screen switched from the HRA seal, which had appeared at the end of the call, to a news alert from channel KOTA, whose large logo swept away as a woman seated behind a desk began to speak.

"We have breaking news to report to you this morning. Luis Ortega, the *DDM TV Live* contestant who disappeared mysteriously during the show's recent hacked broadcast, was found alive and apprehended on a stretch of highway here in South Dakota. We go now to our reporter Gina Byles, who is at Rapid City Regional Hospital where Mr. Ortega is being held for observation. Gina, what can you tell us?"

"Good morning, Barbara. The authorities are being very tight-lipped right now, but the pieces of information we have appear to paint this picture: Mr. Ortega was attempting to flee his Cleveland DDM assignment, and instead return home to Southern California. But the FBI somehow caught wind of his daring escape while he was passing through South

Dakota, and agents successfully conducted an operation to detain him."

"You say it was successful, but if so, why are you speaking to us from a hospital?"

"We in the media have been assured that no harm came to Mr. Ortega during his capture. Authorities say he collapsed due to exhaustion and has been unresponsive ever since. That was ten hours ago. Right now his condition is being monitored by medical personnel."

"Well, assuming that he's going to be okay, what sort of penalties do you think the HRA might impose when he wakes up?"

"That's a good question, Barbara. And perhaps above my pay grade. While some DDM contestants have been known to not give their best effort while on assignment, this may mark the first time someone—let alone a Beneficiary—has gone completely AWOL."

"Thanks for the update, Gina. We'll check back with you as the story develops."

All eyes slowly turned toward Kate after the segment ended. She looked at Jan, who was scrolling through her phone. Before anyone could say a word, the door opened and a man in a dark blue suit walked directly up to Kate.

"We need you on a plane right now. *DDM TV* has chartered the jet. You're going to Rapid City."

"What?" Kate said. "Luis might be in a coma. What could I possibly do to help?"

"The show wants a photo op of you comforting him at his bedside."

Kate was rushed to Teterboro Airport in a private car and arrived in Rapid City four hours later. Another executive car took her directly from the airport to the hospital, and as they pulled up outside she saw a large crowd of people on the sidewalk. Many were holding up posters of Luis's face or signs offering him well wishes. *Where did they come from?* she wondered.

Kate knew that social media had erupted after their episode, with discussions ranging from who was behind the hack to even picking apart the merits of her outfit and makeup. But the most peculiar development was the rise of a sort of Cult of Luis, "the man who dared to defy the HRA."

"Have You Seen Luis?" fan pages appeared and began posting the grainy images they received of young men in skinny jeans that, from the distance at which they were taken, could have been anyone. Three hundred skReacher accounts pretending to be Luis popped up overnight, and ranged from the silly to the perverted to the subversive. Some women even posted topless photos or said they wanted to marry the handsome young man.

But as the days passed with no sign of the reluctant *DDM TV* star, fears of foul play began to circulate. Could the HRA, believing that one of their own employees being sent on assignment was a bridge too far, have hired the CIA to assassinate the young Ortega? What *other* past show participants had the nation not heard from in a while?

Tabloids and entertainment digimags went wild trying to track down the nearly five hundred former contestants, updating their websites by replacing red question marks with green checks next to the faces of those who had been located. The process was bittersweet: while two of the love connections had young babies to show off—"our little peace accord," a proud DDM mother boasted of her daughter—it was found that several Debtors had actually committed suicide since their appearance on the program.

Kate could only assume that this large group outside the hospital had heard that Luis was being held here, and then raced from however far away they lived to greet him when he woke up. Would these people let him go to Cleveland or were they crazy enough to try and help him escape again?

Before she could go down that rabbit hole, some people in the crowd recognized her and started running aggressively toward the car. Kate yelled at the driver to move around whatever was slowing them down, and he lurched the car forward into the garage entrance before any of Luis's fans could harass her.

Once inside the hospital, Kate was escorted upstairs by armed guards, then entered a lobby bustling with staff, news types, and more law enforcement. As she rounded a corner she was mortified to see the shining white teeth of Ryan Richards grinning at her from down the hallway.

"Kate, darling!" he beamed. "I knew you couldn't stay away."

"Hello, Ryan," she said coolly. "I'm glad it's not me in that hospital bed. I doubt you'd be able to control yourself."

"Settle down, you tigress! And don't go committing any DEs against *me* now."

"Whatever. Let's just get this interview over with."

Fifteen minutes later they were led into a private room. Luis was at rest surrounded by soft studio lights and two camera stands. A PA was whispering into the ear of a camera operator, who made a motion toward the nurse adjusting Luis's sheets. Two chairs were brought in and placed near the bed, then Kate and Richards took their places.

"Good day," the host began softly, "Ryan Richards speaking to you at a very somber time. I'm at the bedside of young Luis Ortega, a recent *DDM TV* contestant who's now fighting for his life at a hospital in Rapid City, South Dakota."

The camera panned over and zoomed in onto Luis's face. Without his glasses or hat, he looked even more childlike.

"With me at his side is none other than Kate Donohugh, his twenty-second-degree DDM. Kate," he sighed, "how does it make you feel to see Luis lying there so helplessly?"

"Humbled," she replied. "And reflective. How many times throughout history did one of *my* relatives stand over the body of an Ortega? I'm just so thankful he's alive."

"What's the first thing you want to say to him when he wakes up?"

"That I understand he's scared. But DDM assignments are bigger than us as individuals—we have to make personal sacrifices for the greater good. And it's not just about national healing anymore. There are millions of Victims around the world watching, waiting for their chance at an equitable future."

Richards fell to his knees. "Please, Luis," he begged. "Wake up! You've got to start building those houses!"

After the interview ended, Kate was asked to wait in the reception area because several national reporters who had also flown in were interested in speaking to her. She sat down and grabbed a magazine, flipping through it absently while a wall-mounted TV replayed the interview in front of her. She was about to get up and look for something to drink, when a doctor frantically ran up to the nurses station and pointed at the TV. One of the nurses handed him a remote and he changed the channel to GBC.

Kate set down the magazine and turned her attention to the TV, where a middle-aged man in a gray blazer wearing a dark tactical helmet was squatting behind a car. Speaking into a mic, he said, "Yes, Leslie, I am here outside a warehouse on the east side of Wilmington, Delaware. We received an anonymous tip that SWAT teams were converging on the area, and as you can see, a number of armored trucks and tactical personnel are in place. Now, I've been advised to stay out of the way, but we have reason to believe that this raid may have something to do with the hack on *DDM TV Live* which rocked the nation nearly a week ago, so honestly, I would be doing the viewers a disservice by not bringing them the story as closely as possible in real time."

"Be careful out there, Brent," said a female voice.

"Wait! What's this? Looks like they've breached a roll-up door. Quick! Come on, let's follow them in!"

The picture jerked around as the cameraman ran after the reporter, merging with a stream of officers dressed in tactical gear as they entered the warehouse and fanned out. The picture blurred momentarily before adjusting to the lower light and resolved to reveal an array of computers running down a handful of long folding tables. The sound of voices shouting and metal clanking echoed through the warehouse.

The camera scanned around capturing the action and seconds later the reporter came running up. He removed his helmet and took a big breath, then addressed the camera formally.

"Brent Auburn, reporting live for GBC News, from what sources have just told me is the headquarters of a hacker group calling itself the Sentinels of Jubilee. Only moments ago tactical units gained entry and secured this warehouse. No one is here, there are just rows and rows of computers, each with the name of a different city floating around in the manner of a screen saver. I wonder what would happen if I tapped a key…"

"Hey! What are you doing?"

An officer leaped into frame and grabbed the reporter's arm before he could touch one of the keyboards.

Seconds later the warehouse wall behind them illuminated with the projected image of the same masked man who had interrupted the *DDM TV Live* broadcast. The cameraman adjusted his stance to better frame the wall, then steadied as the projected man spoke.

"Well done, government enforcers! Putting all your toys to good use. But we are still ahead of you and will now lead the way. The computers in front of you are loaded with files and footage from sixty different HRA facilities around the country. How did we get such access?

"Your techs who toil down in the boiler rooms, and who are creating this, the world's largest public works project—they have seen where your ship is headed. Members of law enforcement disgusted by the aggressive measures they are told to employ—they too refuse to keep paving this road to hell. So you see, our movement is not merely populated by disgruntled Debtors, and you dismiss us at your peril.

"For months we have spied on the supervisors, reparaticians, contractors, even some Beneficiaries and Debtors to prove the extent of our reach. Substance abuse in HRA parking lots, employees picking their noses while walking into the restroom, audio of private conversations secretly recorded on both personal and administration devices that were logged into unsecured public wifi networks. Innocent moments, embarrassing moments, and ambiguous moments that are all open to interpretation, misrepresentation, mockery, judgment, and yes, scrutiny.

"Today your ancestors may hang in effigy because of the crumbling documents that survived long enough to be scanned, but tomorrow *you* will be stored in a comprehensive 3D dossier and dissected without context or empathy by future historians, social scientists, judges, and jailers.

"Heaven forbid if science should ever perfect life extension technology or the ability to upload your consciousness—for they will all be waiting to interrogate you, poke you, prod you, humiliate you, sentence your digital avatar to the hellfire of eternal pixel punishment.

"Consider that if God exists, surely He has the decency not to watch while you defecate. We hold no such faith that this amoral juggernaut, which devours data like a crab scavenging the ocean floor for scraps, would ever show such discretion.

"We, the Sentinels of Jubilee, have done everything in our power to warn you about the dangers we all face. Keep your eyes on the screen, and in five minutes it will be *your* turn to take action."

The man flickered out and the picture switched to an elevated view overlooking an exterior parking lot. Text along the bottom of the image said: HRA Field Office – Houston. As two men holding coffee cups walked away from a car, a sophomoric voice mumbled, "So Ted, my daughter blah, blah, blah... Oops!" One of the men stumbled and dropped his cup, which exploded all over his companion's shoes when it hit the ground. The voice cackled hysterically. "Pardon my foible, bro!"

The picture changed again, this time showing the interior of an HRA office in Ft. Lauderdale. A heavyset woman sitting in an interview room tapped a female child on the bottom and motioned for her to sit down. A sportscaster's voice bellowed, "Ooh, a left cross to the backside! That right there is child abuse, my friend." "But Nick," another lively voice said, "did you not see what I saw just moments before the strike (which I have to say was not that hard anyway)? The child ignored repeated verbal requests and warnings to sit still." "Well, Ian. Guess we'll just have to agree to disagree, hyuk hyuk hyuk!"

The scene now switched to the exterior of a building that did not resemble an HRA facility. The text at bottom read: Manhattan Cancer Institute – New York. A young woman stepped outside leaning on the arm of a man. She faltered after taking a few steps. He caught her and helped steady her balance. A moment later she buried her face in his chest and he held her.

A harsh female voice broke in, saying, "Look at this cis scum flaunting their hetero love in public. Disgusting! What about the rest of us and *our* sensibilities? Central, this is Decency Warden 41-18C, reporting two violators of the Public Affection Code, requesting that you deploy Privilege Shields to this location and seize eighteen percent of their assets…"

The screen went black, then the following message slowly appeared:

Is This the Future You Want?
To Learn More Visit:
HRA.gov/Scrutiny

THE END.

BUT THE STORY CONTINUES IN…

REPARATIONS MIND,

REPARATIONS CORE,

& REPARATIONS MAZE.

GLOSSARY

Afrigro-American: American citizen descended from populations originating in the African continent, often brought to the Americas as slaves; term culturally agreed upon as of 2023.

Ambrosia Alert: National child abduction alert system.

Atonement Cream: Popular skincare product known for its soothing properties, inside and out.

Beneficiaries: Members of the Historically Wronged American class, who receive electronic payments from the HRA as compensation for crimes against their ancestors.

Bloodline Crimes: Roll call of confirmed Domination Events committed by a citizen's ancestors.

Book of Reparations: Holy text compiled by left-wing activists during their crusade to create the Historical Reparations Administration.

Burger Citizen: Popular fast food chain specializing in sandwiches, french fries, and soft drinks.

CalmTime: HRA-approved employee time off to recuperate after a stressful half-day at work.

Caucmerican: American citizen descended from populations originating in the European continent; also Cauc (slang, often derogatory).

Certified Historical Event: An occurrence verified by one or more authenticated documents, and included in the MARVIN database timeline.

Citizen Profile: Dossier compiled by MARVIN containing all pertinent personal, historical, criminal, and financial information.

Construction 4 Community: National volunteer organization that builds homes for low-income families.

D Leaves: Slang term, often used mockingly, to refer to MARVIN's monthly data analysis; for example, reading the D leaves.

Debit Score: A numerical expression based on an aggregated analysis of a citizen's historical and lifetime files, calculated monthly by MARVIN.

Debtors: Members of the Legacy Violator class, who reimburse Beneficiaries for ancestral crimes; electronic funds are deducted automatically by the HRA.

Debt Protesters: Informal term applied to Debtors who destroy historical documents in an effort to reduce their monthly Reparations bill.

Decency Warden: Hypothetical law enforcement officer used as a scare tactic during the second Sentinels of Jubilee broadcast.

DDM TV Live: Popular television program created by the HRA as a public forum to clear the bad karma from Direct Descendant Matches.

Dignity Wipe: Illegal removal or obscuring of personally identifying information from security footage recorded at the Mall of Absolution, before its required submission to the federal government.

Direct Descendant Match: Instance where ten or more Domination Events take place between two citizens' bloodlines, known as DDM.

Domination Event: Any affront between two humans, ranging from as little as verbal abuse all the way up to murder; known as a DE.

Extraction Treaty: Diplomatic alliance between the United States and other countries which enables the HRA to collect documents and funds held overseas.

Forgery Level: Metric used by MARVIN while analyzing inauthentic documents submitted via scanner.

Hail Mody: Traditional Modestian prayer seeking to bring about calm, propriety, and discretion.

History Patrol: Law enforcement auxiliary tasked with preventing the destruction of historical documents.

Historical Reparations Administration: National governing body which oversees the collection and distribution of restitution payments; known as the HRA.

HOLA: 2021 immigration law titled Honoring Our Legacy as Americans; referred to derogatorily as Hopefully One Last Amnesty.

Joint Telecom & Penal Bureaus: Recent alliance of two governmental bodies seeking to streamline law enforcement through enhanced communication, surveillance tools, and punishment; known as the JTPB.

Latiz-American: American citizen descended from populations originating in Central and South America, often of mixed Tribal and European ancestry; term culturally agreed upon as of 2022; the male form is Latizo, the female form is Latiza.

Lectrolade: Popular energy drink known for its bright colors, high electrolyte content, and caffeine boost.

Lower Income Retainer Fee: Surcharge added to the monthly bill of many renters across the country; first appeared early in 2028; known as LIRF.

Mall of Absolution: The former Mall of America in Minnesota; home to Modestianity, the religious community led by a former MARVIN team leader known as the Prescient One.

Mantra of Atonement: A popular prayer found within the Book of Reparations.

MARVIN: Macro Aggregating Restitution Vector Input Navigator; the HRA supercomputer whose analysis software calculates citizens' Debit Scores.

Mercies: Anchor chapel in the Mall of Absolution where acolytes go for temporary reprieve from their burdens.

Microscopic Protocol: Proposed variation of the current probation system, as sought by the JTPB.

Minoricans: Any American citizen not of Caucasian or Asian descent.

Noble Gent: Popular malt liquor brand, available in 24 oz cans and 40 oz bottles.

Modestianity: Modern religious sect founded by the Prescient One.

Modidas: Clothing manufacturer with exclusive license to all branded apparel sold at the Mall of Absolution.

Nifty Minutes: Weekly newsmagazine television program that reports on politics and topical social issues.

One Match Strike and You're Out Law: Strict sentencing guidelines established in 2027 to discourage citizens from destroying historical documents as an attempt to reduce their Debit Score.

Pardon My Foible: Slang expression, often sarcastic, used by teenagers to comment on a mistake or accident.

Pleasantry Station: Any number of attractions within the Mercies anchor chapel at the Mall of Absolution that enables a person to temporarily relieve the burdens of one's guilt.

Predator Predator Network: Nationwide surveillance system targeting human traffickers.

The Prescient One: Founder of Modestianity, a modern religious sect based out of the Mall of Absolution.

Privacy Shield: Hypothetical law enforcement tool used as a scare tactic during the second Sentinels of Jubilee broadcast.

Public Affection Code: Hypothetical ordinance used as a scare tactic during the second Sentinels of Jubilee broadcast.

Reparatician: Highly specialized document examiner trained to identify forgeries.

Reparations: United States law passed in 2025 that established the HRA, which oversees the collection and dispensation of compensatory payments to citizens descended from victims of slavery and colonialism.

Reparations Evading Tactical Collectors: Paramilitary force entrusted by the HRA with discretionary powers in apprehending suspects, preserving documents, and seizing assets; known as the RETC.

Reparology: Comprehensive, cross-disciplinary college-level curriculum designed to prepare students for HRA careers.

SafePlace: Sophisticated document scanners installed in home fireplaces, as mandated by the 2026 executive order.

Scrutiny State: Term coined by the Prescient One referring to his doomsday prediction of total surveillance.

Sentinels of Jubilee: Underground anti-HRA resistance group accused of hacking into the MARVIN computer database.

Sift n' Scan: Patented scanning technology and equipment installed in History Patrol drones to efficiently secure, preserve, and scan partially destroyed historical documents, usually by fire.

skReacher: Messaging app where users communicate by posting short blurbs.

S'more Stoppers: Nickname given to History Patrol drones that assist in document preservation and non-lethal suspect neutralization.

State Appointed Digital Attorney: Computer-generated legal counsel offered free of charge; known as a SADA.

Stigmatized Relics: Politically incorrect possessions from past cultural eras, often kept for symbolic reasons; their legality varies.

TapOut: Internal HRA computer program used by employees when signing in to CalmTime.

Tears: Penance-themed anchor chapel in the Mall of Absolution.

Thinkings Institution: Public policy research organization based in Washington, DC.

Tribal American: Descendant of the original indigenous populations which inhabited North, Central, and South America prior to European colonization.

War for Equity: Political movement spearheaded by left-wing change agents seeking to level the playing field for historically oppressed groups.

The Zap: Storefront in the Mall of Absolution which hosts interracial healing sessions.

ABOUT THE AUTHOR

Originally from Northern Virginia, Philip Wyeth has lived in the Los Angeles area for many years. He's an entrepreneur, musician, film aficionado, hockey fan, and enjoys playing tennis and golf.

Inspired by such unique writers as Heinrich von Kleist, Ambrose Bierce, Joseph Conrad, and Len Deighton, Wyeth's imaginative novels will resonate with fans of Philip K. Dick, Rich Larson, Michel Houellebecq, and Neal Stephenson.

Also a lifelong fan of heavy metal music and its many sub-genres, Wyeth strives to infuse his writing with comparable levels of intensity, independence, and larger-than-life visions.

His website is www.philipwyeth.com, and you can follow him across the social media landscape under the following handles:

@PhilipWyeth: Twitter, BitChute, Gab, and Minds.

@PhilipWyethWriter: Instagram and Facebook.